The Dragon Chronicles™

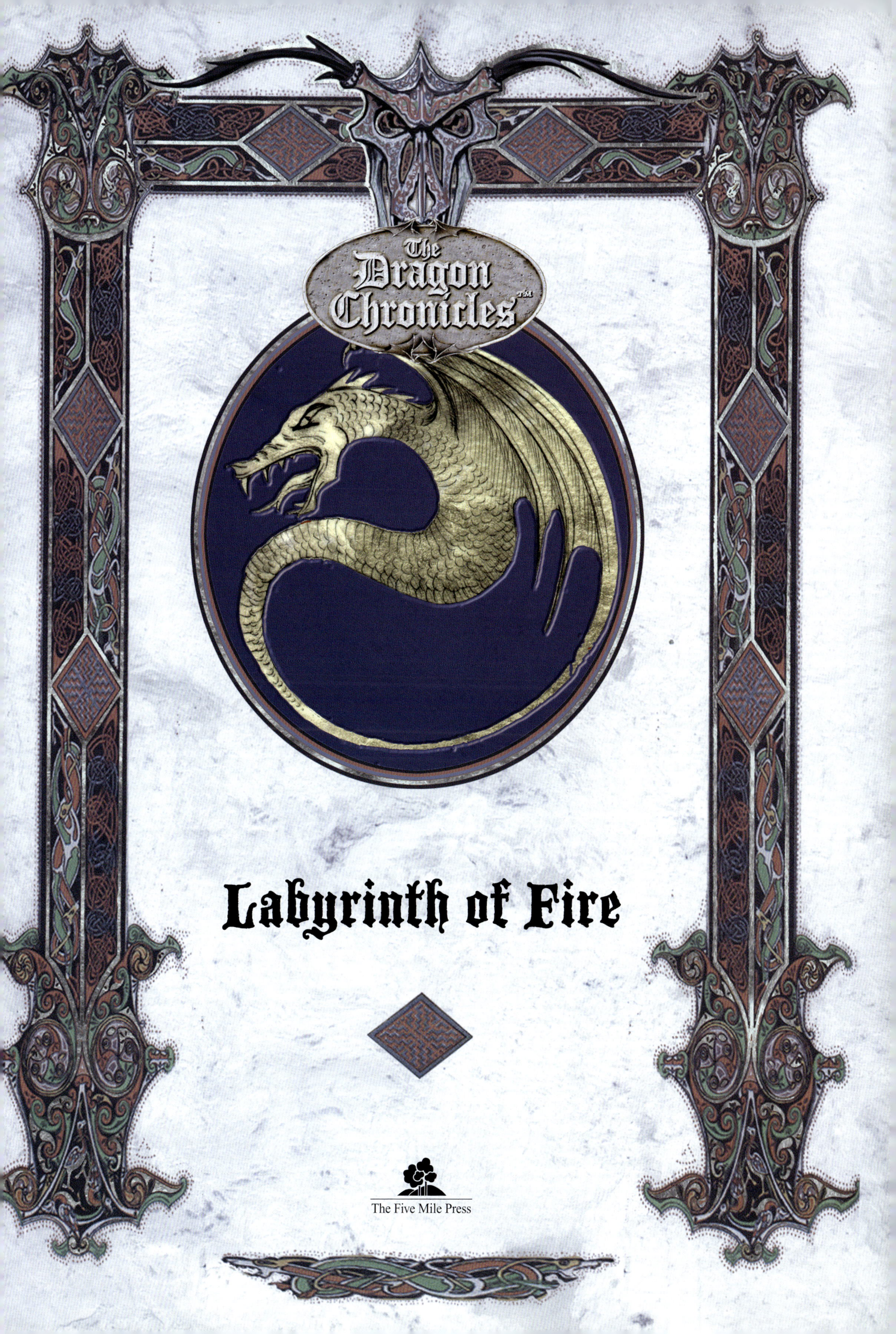

Labyrinth of Fire

The Five Mile Press

The Five Mile Press Pty Ltd
1 Centre Road, Scoresby
Victoria 3179 Australia
www.fivemile.com.au

The Dragon Chronicles is a trade mark owned by Meiklejohn Graphics
Text and illustrations copyright © Meiklejohn Graphics
Illustrations by Jan Patrik Krasny
Story by Claire Hawcock
Edited by Chris Meiklejohn
Art Direction by Chris and Pauline Meiklejohn
www.dragonchronicles.com

All rights reserved under the Pan-American and International Copyright Conventions

First published 2011

Printed in China   5 4 3 2 1

This book may not be reproduced in whole or in part, in any form or by any means, electronic or mechanical, including photocopying, recording, or any information storage and retrieval system now known or hereafter invented, without written permission from the publisher.

Contents

Chapter One
Storm Clouds Gather

Chapter Two
The Gift

Chapter Three
Under Attack

Chapter Four
Might and Magic

Chapter Five
Darkness and Light

Chapter Six
Trapped

Chapter Seven
A Warning

Chapter Eight
The Labyrinth of Fire

Chapter Nine
The Search for Truth

Chapter Ten
Dark Magic

Chapter Eleven
Mortal Danger

Chapter Twelve
Kingship and Kin

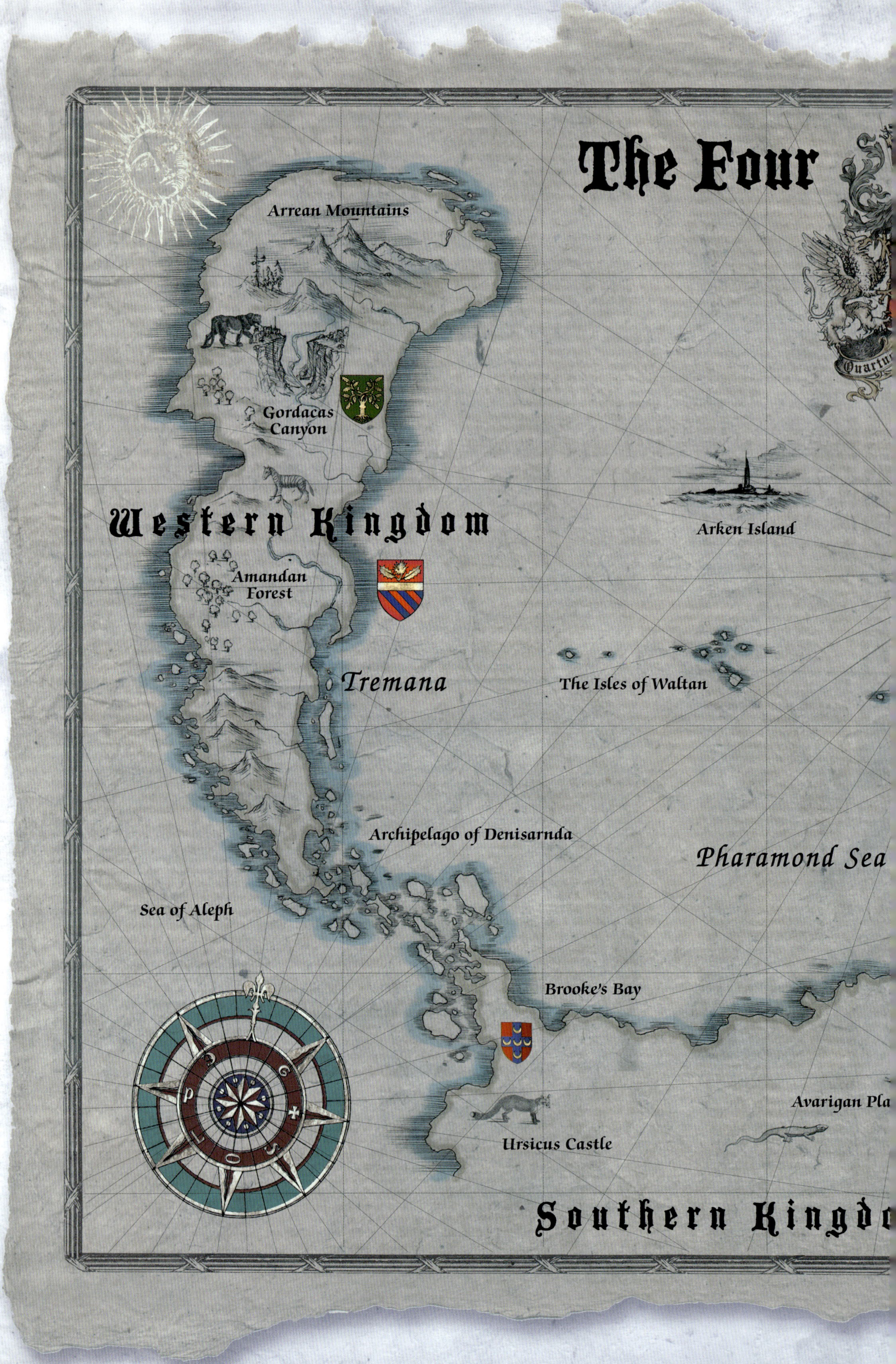

The Four
Arrean Mountains
Gordacas Canyon
Western Kingdom
Amandan Forest
Arken Island
Tremana
The Isles of Waltan
Archipelago of Denisarnda
Pharamond Sea
Sea of Aleph
Brooke's Bay
Avarigan Pla
Ursicus Castle
Southern Kingd

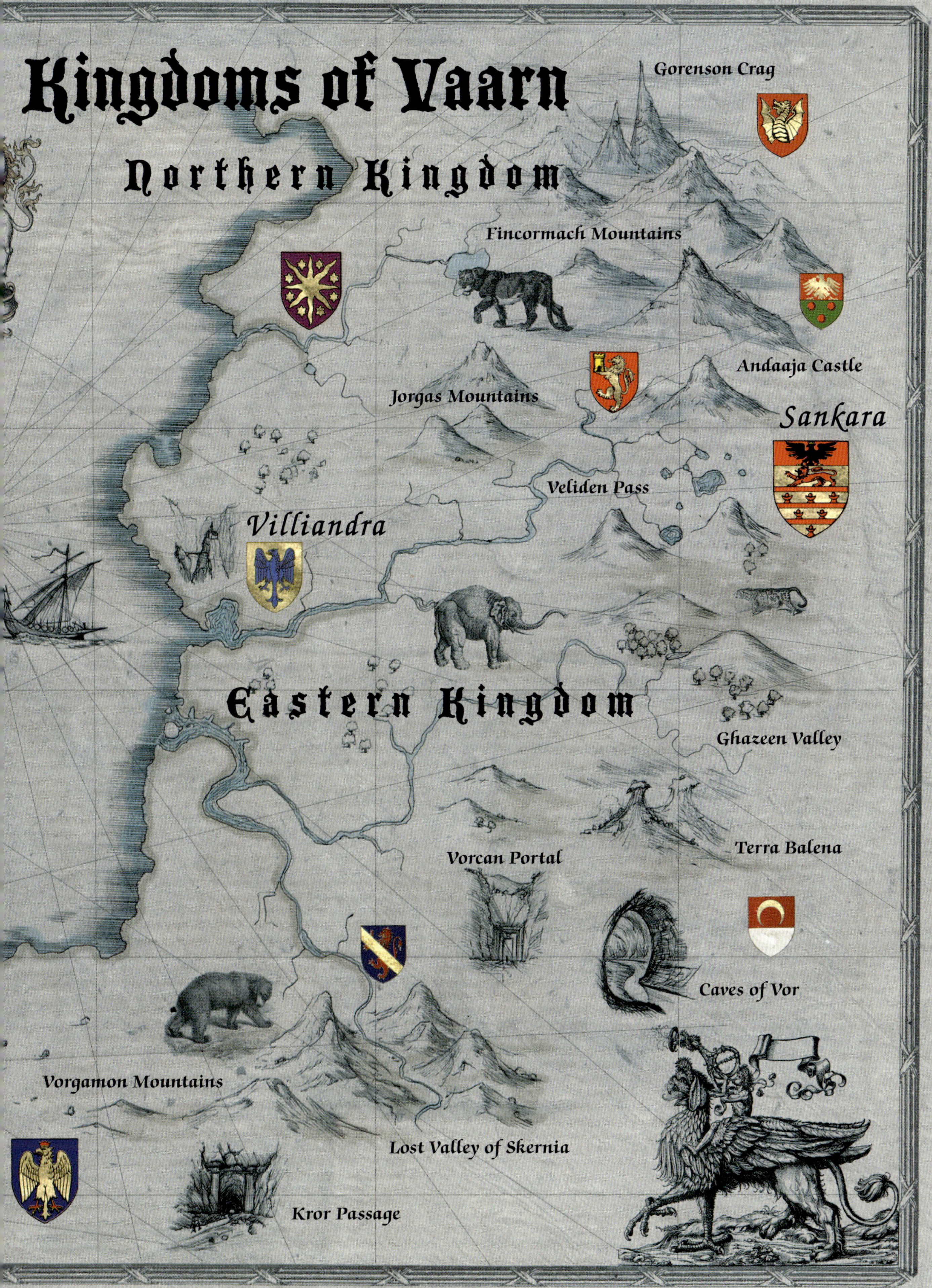
Kingdoms of Vaarn
Northern Kingdom
Gorenson Crag
Fincormach Mountains
Andaaja Castle
Jorgas Mountains
Sankara
Veliden Pass
Villiandra
Eastern Kingdom
Ghazeen Valley
Terra Balena
Vorcan Portal
Caves of Vor
Vorgamon Mountains
Lost Valley of Skernia
Kror Passage

I can recall the first attack quite clearly — the sights, smells and sounds of those few hours are still with me even though they took place over half a century ago. Perhaps this is because it happened in my youth — a time during which we live more intensely than any other; then again, perhaps it is simply because the event marked the end of mine.

Over the years, I have preferred not to dwell on the fearsome acts that followed. But lately, forced through illness to take to my bed, I have increasingly been drawn into dark memories of my mind. Memories that bring nightmares to my sleeping hours and, during daylight, a growing need to tell my tale.

The account that follows is a faithful record of the attack and ensuing adventure. It is a sequel to a journal that documents the great wizard Septimus Angorius' struggles and, like the first, will hopefully serve as testament to the brave efforts made to protect us from the evil that inhabits the dark corners of our land. It is also the story of the making of a king.

Chapter One

Storm Clouds Gather

It was an hour or two before sunset and a glorious afternoon. Down at the shore a gentle wind blew off the land, causing just a few foamy tips to form on the Pharamond Sea. Together with my younger brother Alvah, I was spending the afternoon racing stallions along the shore. I remember looking up above our party at the palace beyond the forest. Built before I was born by my father, I still hardly believed that I, Bandred di Sandorius, King of the Four Kingdoms of Vaarn, had guardianship of this impressive place. That day, framed by the imposing heights of the Jorgas Mountains, the palace stood in all its glory — its warm sandstone walls wrapping us in its protective glow.

Then suddenly the light was gone. In its place darkness grew and with it a slight chill. At first I thought, as I am sure my courtiers did, that raintime had arrived early; that soon the many days of driving rain and blasting winds would force us, as they did every year, to retreat inside the palace walls. I looked out to where sea and sky met and, sure enough, storm clouds were gathering, blocking out the sun. Strangely, the sea was calm. I signalled to the stablemen to gather the horses, frustrated that our afternoon's sport had come to an end. The horses, however, were unsettled and in no mood to respond. Some were whinnying, shaking their heads and stepping from side to side as if some small creature was snapping at their heels. Others seemed angry, snorting hot breath through arched nostrils and stamping their strong forelegs. Those secured to posts were trying to break free, pulling back and forth on their bridles, their bits sliding around their salivating mouths like oars thrusting in and out of a restless sea. They seemed distracted and were not consoled by the horsemen's gentle words. Finally, one broke away and galloped off towards the forest, scattering the set and causing much excitement amongst our party.

I glanced up once again at the palace, now flat and lifeless in the darkness, and then out to sea. It was then that horror struck. What loomed before us, I could hardly comprehend. A leviathan monster, featureless and dark, was flying towards the shore. Fear overwhelmed me and I started to run. Alvah and the rest of the party, having observed the monstrosity, followed suit. We all ran full pelt across the sand towards the forest path, abandoning the horses, believing that our only chance of survival was to take cover in the palace. Half running, half stumbling we moved along the knotted path, blowing horns and shouting warnings in the hope that the palace guards would hear our cries.

As I looked back towards the shore, the creature seemed to have grown, and gave the impression that some parts of its body were moving more rapidly than others. I kept running, the blood that was racing through my body forcing me forward. And as I ran, the full horror of our assailant began to take shape. This was not one single creature but hundreds, possibly thousands of smaller ones, and I had encountered them before. They were dragons, possessed dragons, whose vicious attacks we had not endured since the evil wizard Ganzicus was destroyed ten years ago. Here they were again in full force – their mission to destroy our Kingdoms' peace.

I was exhausted but with all the strength I could muster, I forced myself onwards. I knew that if we reached the palace confines we would not be so exposed. But it was too late. The skies were thick with creatures and soon the first of them were upon us. As the cloud above us burst, the attack began, and a mass of legless, bat-winged serpents, all hideous jaws and barbed tails let forth their piercing whines, a sound that flooded my ears and probed every channel of my brain. Struggling to focus, I was brought to by the sight of the courtiers on their knees with their hands pressed firmly over their ears; their faces crumpled with pain.

From high above, a swarm of tiny dragonets showered us with burning poison. I took cover only to see a flock of dragons with huge umbrellas of leathery black wings and vast coiled trunks flying overhead. Heading straight for the palace guards who were stationed along the battlements, the creatures used their sharp talons to pluck each of the poor men high into the air before releasing them to their horrible deaths below.

I forged ahead of my party and ran up Hundred Steps Passage towards the South Tower door. Inside the palace there was chaos. Many of its inhabitants lay injured and writhing in pain on the ground. Other brave men, having armed themselves, were standing in the open courtyard, horribly exposed to the onslaught of venom and burning flames that rained down on them. Shooting arrows blindly into the air, they had little chance of halting the attack. People were running in all directions not knowing whether to seek cover or seize their weapons, which now seemed powerless against the thick blanket of evil that had gathered over the rooftops. The scene was chaos. Some dragons were flying with no regard for their own lives into the spires. This caused blocks of stone to tumble down onto anything and everyone below.

People, terrified of being crushed to death, were retreating, with only a brave few staying to defend the main entrances. More than once I saw the smaller dragonets swoop down and try to break through.

Not knowing which way to turn, something above the East Tower caught my eye. A vast, scaled dragon hovered with intent, spitting high-speed shafts of fire that reduced each of its victims to a pile of smouldering bones. As the billows of smoke cleared, I saw that it was harnessed – its hooded rider, the evil Count Veldspar, powerful wizard and ruler of Svaal, alighting on the battlements below.

I realised at that moment what he had come for and, without delay, took the shortest route to the East Tower door. I slipped inside and, leaving my warriors to defend the palace, rushed down the tower stairs to the vaults. Two guards lay dead at the door but I had no time to ponder their loss. As soon as I reached the table at the end of the room,

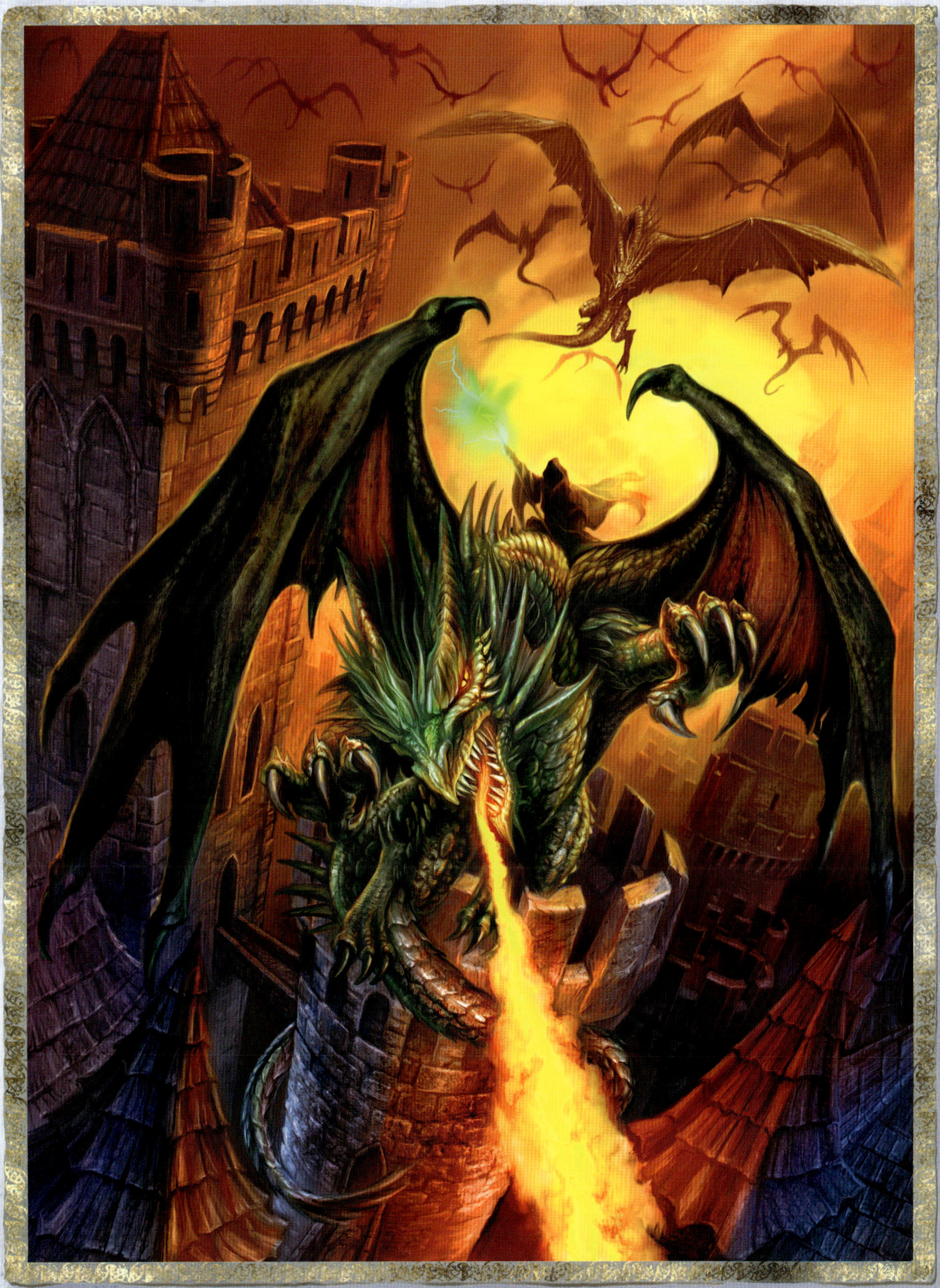

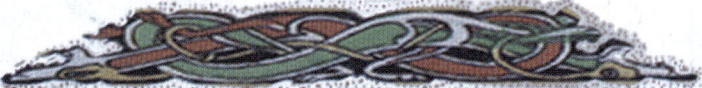

Count Veldspar Attacks!

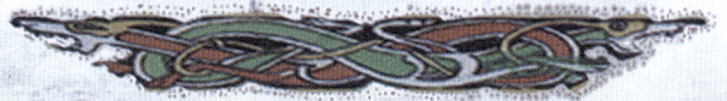

an intense pain seared through my right shoulder. A stray dragonet had followed and was now clamped onto me, its venomous talons gripping my burning skin.

I knew enough about these creatures to act quickly. I reached for my knife and, in one swift movement, released it from its sheath and started, with wild abandon, to slash the savage creature. The dragonet's claws released and, taking my chance, I hurried towards the alcove at the far end of the room. Reaching the gold casket, I threw off the lid and took out the leather-bound book inside. Ripping off the clasp, I turned to the back cover. Inside a small velvet-lined recess rested the legendary Sankara Amulet. A glowing radiance emanated from the huge turquoise stone.

Used for centuries in times of need by Vaarnian wizards and sorceresses, the Amulet provided a channel to a higher power, and for a short while I was quite entranced. Slowly, I became aware that the hall was full of the sound of flapping wings and eager to remove the Amulet from the tower vault and out of Count Veldspar's reach, I pulled off the protective brace and grasped the precious stone.

As the swarm of dragonets approached, I drew my sword, thrusting it this way and that with abandonment, slashing wings and puncturing bodies. But, however many I killed, the creatures kept on coming. I was outnumbered and outmatched and although I continued to fight I knew I had lost. Finally, with the creatures snapping at my arms and legs and clawing at my clothes and hair, I was forced to lie face down on the floor. I feared for my life at that moment, but then, as suddenly as the dragonets had appeared, they retreated. I lifted my head. In their place Count Veldspar stood above me – the Amulet in his hand and a self-satisfied grimace on his face.

If I had feared for my life before, I knew that it was over now.

'On your knees, head down,' he growled, raising his sword high into the air.

I froze. Was this how I was to die? Beheaded and then paraded for all to see? Count Veldspar barked the order again and kicked me hard, forcing my head to the ground. I tensed, expecting the blow; instead I heard a cry. When I looked up, my brother Alvah and a group of soldiers were wielding swords and axes to fight off the dragonets. Alvah had struck Count Veldspar, who, bleeding heavily from his shoulder, was making a hasty retreat towards the stairs that led to the tower roof. Jumping to my feet I followed fast behind, anxious to retrieve the Amulet. I arrived just in time to see Count Veldspar climbing up onto his dragon. He turned and fixed his gaze on me.

'Prepare for your death,' he rasped. 'Your Kingdoms *will* be mine.' Grasping a horn from his saddle, he put it to his lips. A low rumble echoed around the stonework and suddenly the dragons were off – their mission complete, my reputation destroyed and the power of the Amulet in the grip of one of the most evil men our land had ever known.

With the retreat, an eerie silence pervaded the palace broken only by the intermittent screams of the injured and the pitiful weeping of those whose loved-ones had been killed. Quickly and silently, those of us who were able set to work alongside the palace physician. We toiled into the night, offering comfort where we could. I felt great sadness as body after body was carried either to the Great Hall, where a temporary sanatorium had been set up, or to the makeshift mortuary in the vaults below. Time and time again, I marvelled at the resolve of the people. The bravery of the victims was admirable. One poor soul, buried by a stack of rubble, barely alive but conscious begged his rescuers not to spend their time retrieving him but to use their strength to save others. Another man, appallingly burned by the dragons' poison, battled all night with unimaginable pain, and yet he bore it quietly. It was humbling to observe.

But the burden of this heavy work did nothing to quell the dark thoughts I harboured in my mind. These were my people, they were my responsibility and I had failed them. For five whole years I had played at being King, using my privileged position to exact the most enjoyment it is possible for a young man to experience. And despite the numerous warnings of Count Veldspar's skirmishes, I had left others to make the important decisions of state, while I revelled in the luxury of my birthright.

It was too dark to view the damage to the palace, but even then I knew it would break my heart to see. This place was in my blood. It was my father's vision, a legacy he wished to pass on to me and to future generations of the Sandorius family. And what of the Amulet? Possessed by my family for over three hundred years, its unique power was now in the grip of evil. I had to ask myself the question: how was it that I had allowed this to happen? And so, later that night, unable to sleep, I turned to Lord Dedren, my guardian and my father's younger brother, to provide the answer. He was, as ever, supportive, if not a little dismissive of my concerns.

'Do not blame yourself so absolutely,' Lord Dedren softly advised. 'Did you not send *me* to the East with the express demand of suppressing the uprisings?'

'More your request than my demand,' I responded, remembering how little regard I had paid to events unfolding in the furthest reaches of our Kingdoms.

'You are young Bandred and know little of the workings of state. Remember, I have spent many valuable years alongside your father and am happy to assist you in your reign.'

I did remember. For decades our family had been in conflict with Count Veldspar of Svaal and his dark land that lay to the east of our Kingdoms. During the latter years of my father's reign, Count Veldspar's army had started to make inroads: a village here, a town there; until eventually the Svaalians had started to threaten the stability of the region. Using both the expertise of his military commander, Captain Kronson, and his own unrivalled skill of diplomacy, my father had put an end to the advancements. A boundary agreement setting out a large neutral territory had been drawn up and the borders closed. All further communication had been severed. However, early this year there had been reports that this neutral territory was, once again, inhabited. Count Veldspar, taking advantage of my father's death and my relative inexperience, had rescinded the agreement. Lord Dedren had offered to deal with the matter. Together with Captain Kronson – who was sadly lost in the battle – and several hundred warriors, he quashed the renegades and returned home with nothing but reports of success. I was much in his debt.

'In the five years of my reign, I have relied heavily on you, Lord Dedren. Some may say, too heavily,' I said.

'I offer my support and you are wise to take it,' he replied. 'There was certainly nothing that could have prepared us for this dreadful attack. Go to bed, sleep and tomorrow we shall decide what we should do.'

His resolute words that once would have soothed my conscience and calmed my nerves, that night, did nothing to quell the feeling of dread I held in my heart. Still greatly troubled I returned to my bedchamber, not for the first time wishing that my dear father were here to take command.

Chapter Two

The Gift

The following day I rose before dawn and, taking care not to wake my servant, Gurin, made my way down to the palace cemetery. This secluded garden, tucked away to the west of the Main Tower and enclosed within the age-old arms of a dozen stately oak trees, is the resting place for generations of the Sandorius family. For centuries the tombs were barely visible beneath the annual advancement of unbridled growth. However, when my father rebuilt the palace he lavished special attention on this site, clearing the ground and surrounding it with an ornate stone wall, which in turn became clothed in sweet-smelling roses. It became a haven for a multitude of insects and, as a child, I was fascinated by this place, struck by the fact that this abundance of life on the surface belied those that lay dead and lifeless underneath.

As the only key-holder, I locked the gate behind me, ensuring I would be undisturbed for the important ritual I was to perform. Many years before, I had been shown how, in times of need, I might draw upon the wisdom of my ancestors. Indeed, it was my father who had instructed me in this invocation of the spirits, the same spirits he had called on himself before the defeat of Ganzicus and the dragons. Now, taking a leather wrap from my sack, I carefully unravelled it to reveal the sacred tools I hoped would help direct me in my task. Inside was a musical pipe fashioned from a dragon's bone and two charred sticks said to have come from the ancient ash, found in the forests to the north of Villiandra.

Sitting at the foot of my father's grave, I began the ceremony, first slotting the smaller stick into a well-worn hole in the larger one and then rolling it back and forth through the palms of my hands. As I worked, I thought back to the man who had first introduced me to the art of making fire – Septimus Angorius, once wizard to the court and my father's lifelong friend. In my infancy he had first shown me this seemingly miraculous act, I had wondered at the spectacle, especially when after the first few sparks had leapt into more solid flames, he worked his magic to turn them into a moving gallery of miniature animals that danced about and flickered in the air. My interest in wizardry was roused that day, so much so that during my childhood I secretly harboured the hope that one day Septimus might take me as his apprentice. But the years told I had not the calling, and when my childhood friend, Amaleh di Varian had shown her talents, she was indeed the natural choice.

My thoughts were interrupted when suddenly the spluttering sparks at the base of the sticks burst into flame. Blowing gently to extinguish the fire, a thread of smoke climbed first one way, then the other, until dispersing and filling my head with its musky scent. I picked up the pipe and pressing it to my lips started to play, willing to receive the sounds and smells that had travelled across a thousand years. After a while I was lost in the experience and although my hands were still, on and on the music played. Gradually, the garden danced into life as ghostly forms drifted up from the tombs, unrecognisable at first then seemingly human, before fading and disappearing into thin air.

During my initiation I had been taught not to ask questions but merely to be open to whatever was offered. Today I found this difficult. Over and over I wanted to ask what I should do; again and again I needed an answer. Suddenly, the shapes seemed to be coming thick and fast. They were closing in and I felt a chill as they brushed past me. The scent from the smoke was overpowering. I felt dizzy, and then I must have blacked out.

When I awoke it was warm and light. Then I sensed something was different, there was a charge, a feeling of energy in the air. The sun was rising, but this was more powerful: a light that almost blinded me with its brilliance. Then, as the intolerable brightness faded, I saw a white horse from which a woman stepped down. I knew in an instant who it was. As my eyes grew accustomed to the light I realised that it was not a horse she had been riding but a magnificent unicorn.

'Amaleh?' I whispered. She nodded. I was amazed at what she had become. Not my spirited friend – the girl I had waved off with Septimus ten years ago – but a woman alive with magical energy; a sorceress with powers I could hardly imagine. I looked at her that day as if for the first time: pale red hair threaded with strands of gold, shimmering as they caught the light; clear blue eyes, full of knowledge, holding me steadfastly in their gaze; and a grace that conveyed a sense of inner peace rarely found in one so young. I admit I was entranced by the vision of her and when she spoke, so full were my eyes with her beauty, I barely heard a word of what she said.

'Have you lost your tongue as well as your mind Bandred?' she continued, snapping me out of my reverie.

I recovered myself and stood up, 'Welcome, Amaleh, you are most warmly received.'

'Do not waste your breath on formalities, Bandred,' she replied, 'I am not here as your servant, but to retrieve the heritage of the magic world. As the only notable feat of your reign so far, the loss of the Sankara Amulet is a particularly spectacular one. What exactly are you proposing to do about it?'

Her harsh words stung me and I found myself struggling to respond, 'I have spoken to Lord Dedren ...'

'Lord Dedren,' she interrupted, 'is not responsible for the matters of state, Bandred, you are. What plans have *you* made?'

Infuriatingly, I knew that she was right, but I was outraged. How dare she talk to me in such a disrespectful way? I had deliberately not requested Amaleh's presence because I had wanted to discuss the matter

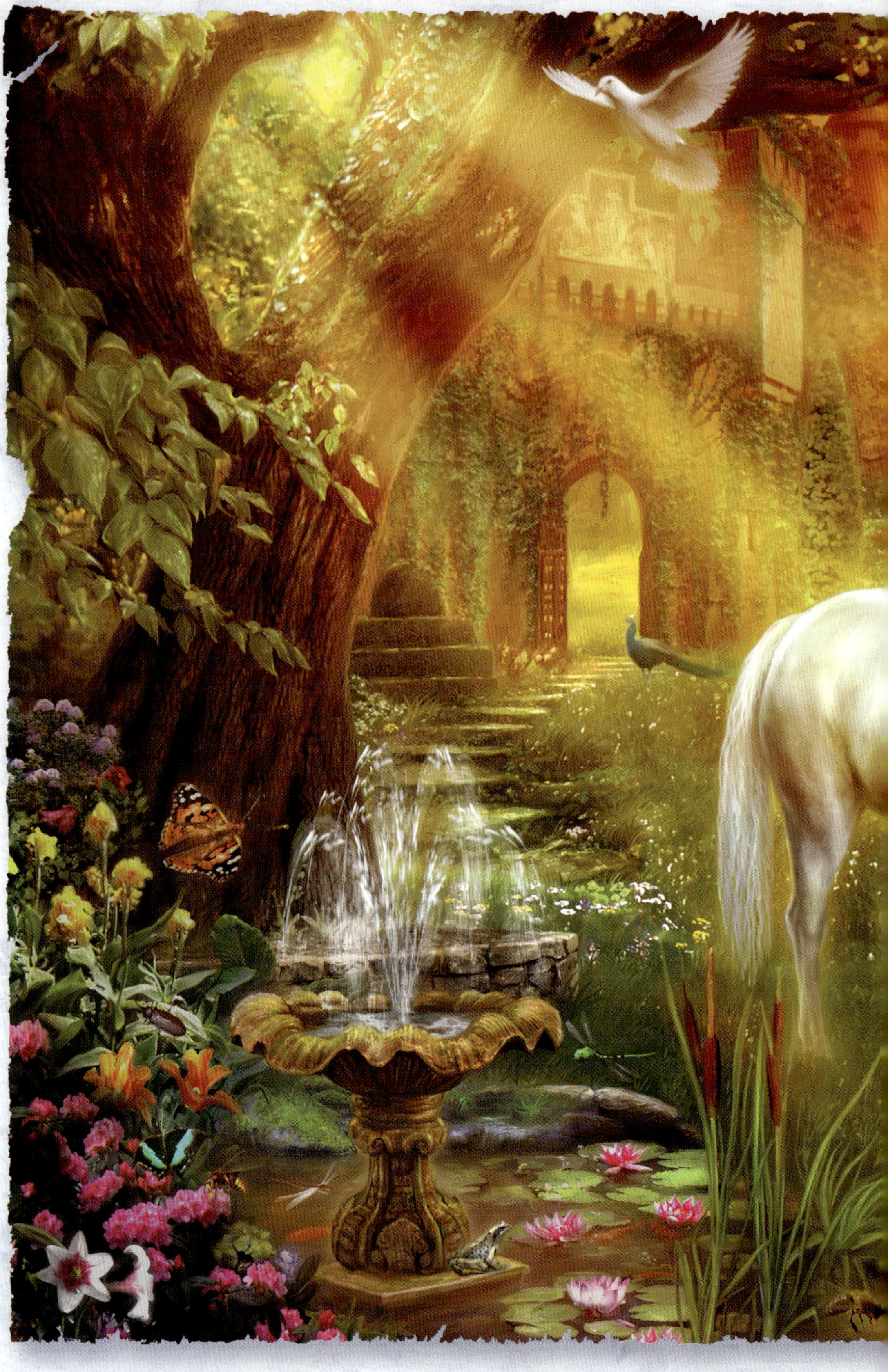

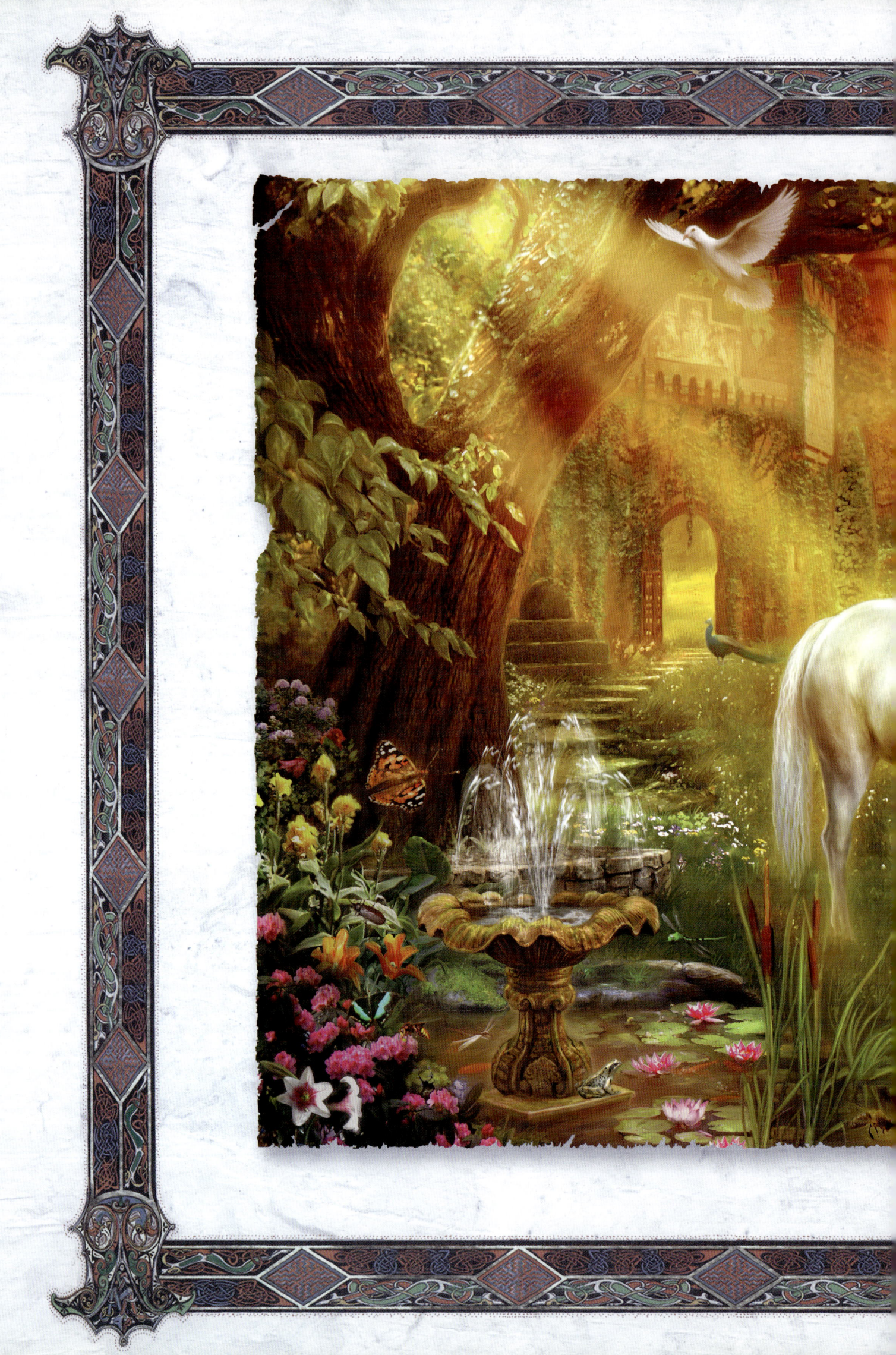

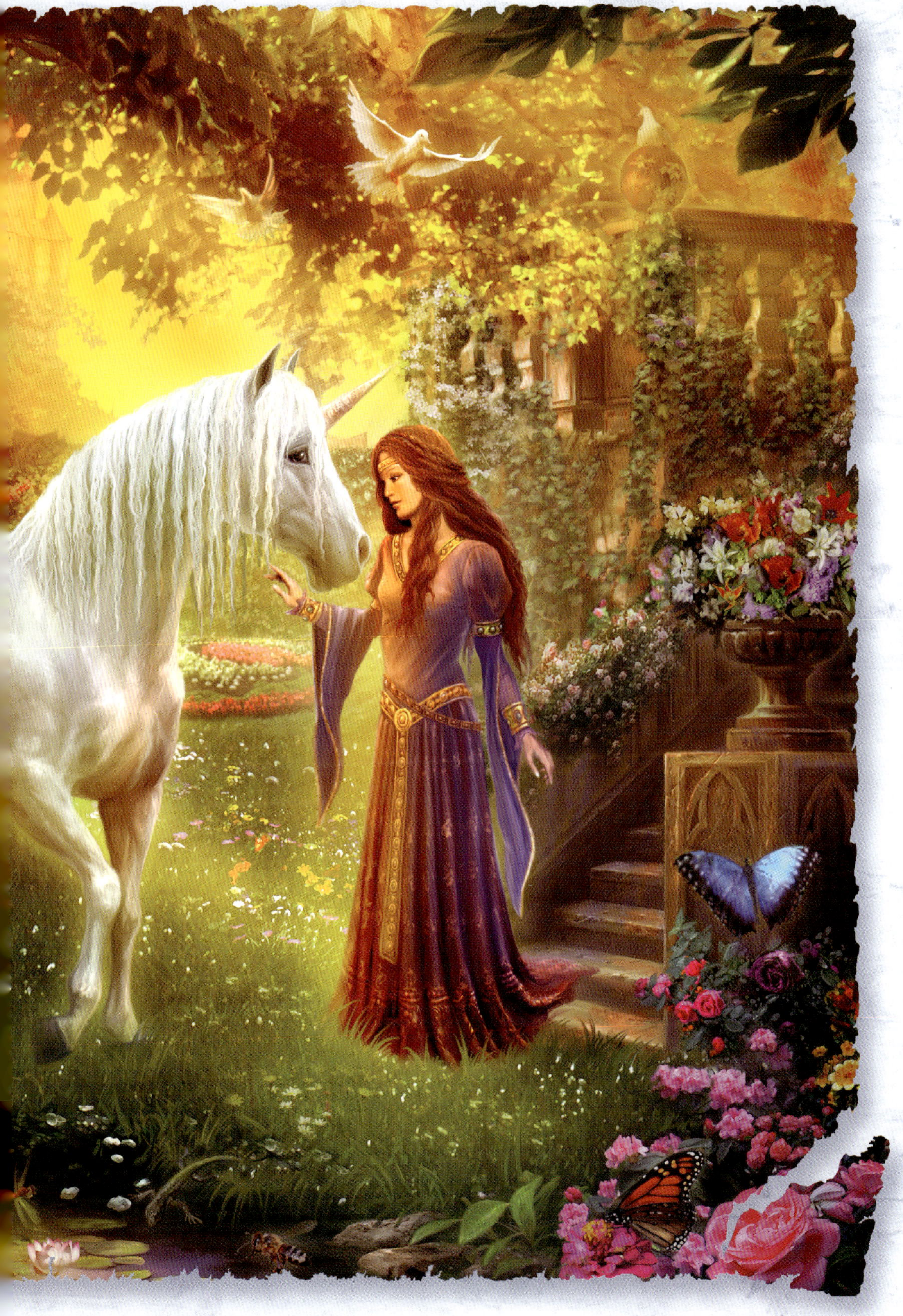

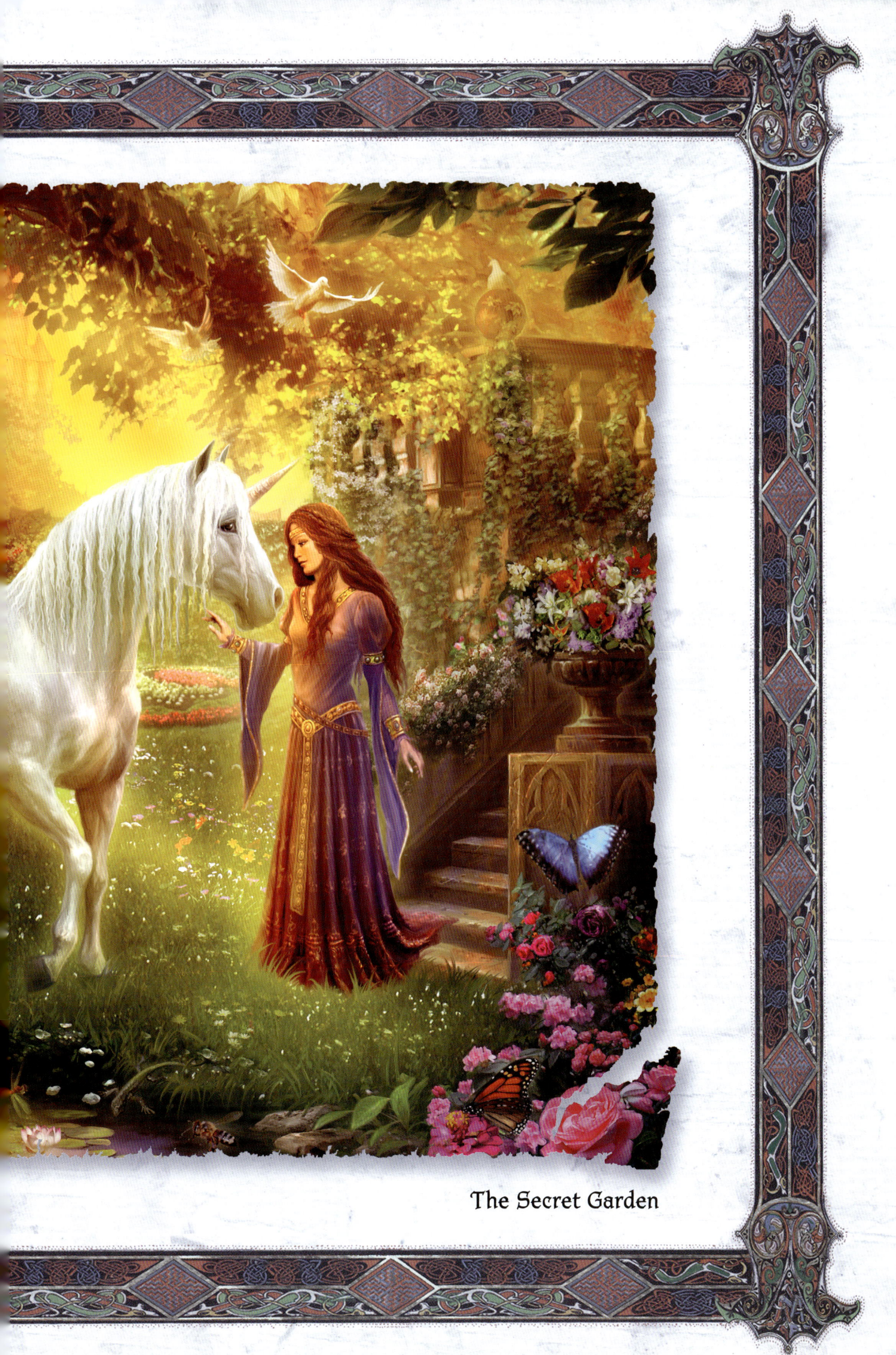

The Secret Garden

with the High Council first. Now, although angered by her accusation, I was forced to defend myself and so, again, I attempted a response.

'Since the last malevolent assault against our Kingdoms, there have been five years of relative peace. Therefore, despite the recent border battles with Svaal, I was reluctant to mount an occupation. I realise now that I may have been mistaken, but this attack was completely unexpected. The loss of the Sankara Amulet is a deep regret and I will do everything in my power to retrieve it.'

She moved closer and as she did I felt her power again. I thought back to the times we had spent together as children under Septimus' watchful eye and marvelled at this transformation. Her talent had grown over the years under his apprenticeship and, despite her disdain, I had to admire her obvious dedication to the art of magic.

'Here, Bandred,' she offered in her hand a sealed letter. 'Septimus gave me this before he left. He instructed me to pass it on to you if ever there was another threat made against the Kingdoms. I suggest you read it and perhaps then you shall find it a little easier to make a decision.'

And before I could ask any questions, she had mounted the unicorn and, clearing the wall with an effortless jump, disappeared into the mist.

Back at the palace the daily bustle had begun, and while Amaleh settled into her chambers, those reserved for the Supreme Wizard or Sorceress serving the Court, I retired to my private quarters to study the letter. Written in the hand I recognised as that of my father's dear friend and once Wizard to the Court, Septimus Angorius, this is what it said:

My dearest Bandred,

As well you know, I have spent nigh on three hundred years in the service of your esteemed family and I will be deeply sad to leave. During that time I have been witness to many extraordinary happenings, some good, some evil, but it is without a doubt that the most progress the Four Kingdoms has enjoyed was during your father's reign. Despite numerous trials and tribulations, Vaarn is stronger now than it has ever been. What you may or may not know, however, is that during the conflict with Ganzicus, I exhausted my powers. Unable to restore my energies, due, no doubt, to my advanced years, it is with regret that I now must retreat and endure 'The Fading', the process that, in time, becomes every magi's fate.

    Tomorrow marks the beginning of suntime, the day on which I have the lamentable occasion to depart my house at Villiandra and consign my long-held position as Supreme Wizard to the young and gifted sorceress, Amaleh di Varian. I leave at sunrise and plan to visit you at the Palace to pay my final respects prior to travelling North to the Palace of the Elders in Gorenson, but before I do so I will give Amaleh this letter for safekeeping. The knowledge held within is extremely valuable and under no circumstances and at no time must it fall into the hands of our enemies.

    After the last great battle, which was against the turned wizard, Ganzicus, I feared that if ever an evil more powerful than his could command the dragons and attempt another assault on our Kingdoms, it would be almost impossible to defeat. It is difficult to imagine the unfathomable depths to which pure evil can plunge, but I knew that if I could spare you this, it would offer me great comfort in my final days. And so, Bandred, as is tradition, I should like to leave you with a gift.

There is an ancient book, older than 'The Book of Serafan', of which you may have heard. This book, passed on through generations of wizards and sorceresses, is called 'The Supernatural History of the Kingdoms of Vaarn'. As its name dictates, it records every supernatural creature in Vaarn known to man. Scribed within are hundreds upon thousands of entries: some detailed and supported by elaborate sketches; others offering just a line or two of words. On my return, I studied this book and found what I had been looking for: a mythical creature I had first heard of many years ago, but, despite travelling widely throughout the Four Kingdoms, had never the occasion to encounter. This is the entry, made many centuries ago by a wizard in service during the days of one of your ancestors:

Draco labyrintia – not of solid matter but intermittently taking the shape of a four-legged, winged dragon. Habitat: underground labyrinth that through a pool-filled cavern leads to a ring of fire. Dimensions: 50 feet in length and width. Physical characteristics: almost imperceptible but include a long and protruding mandible distinguished by two horned nostrils and two sets of fanged teeth,

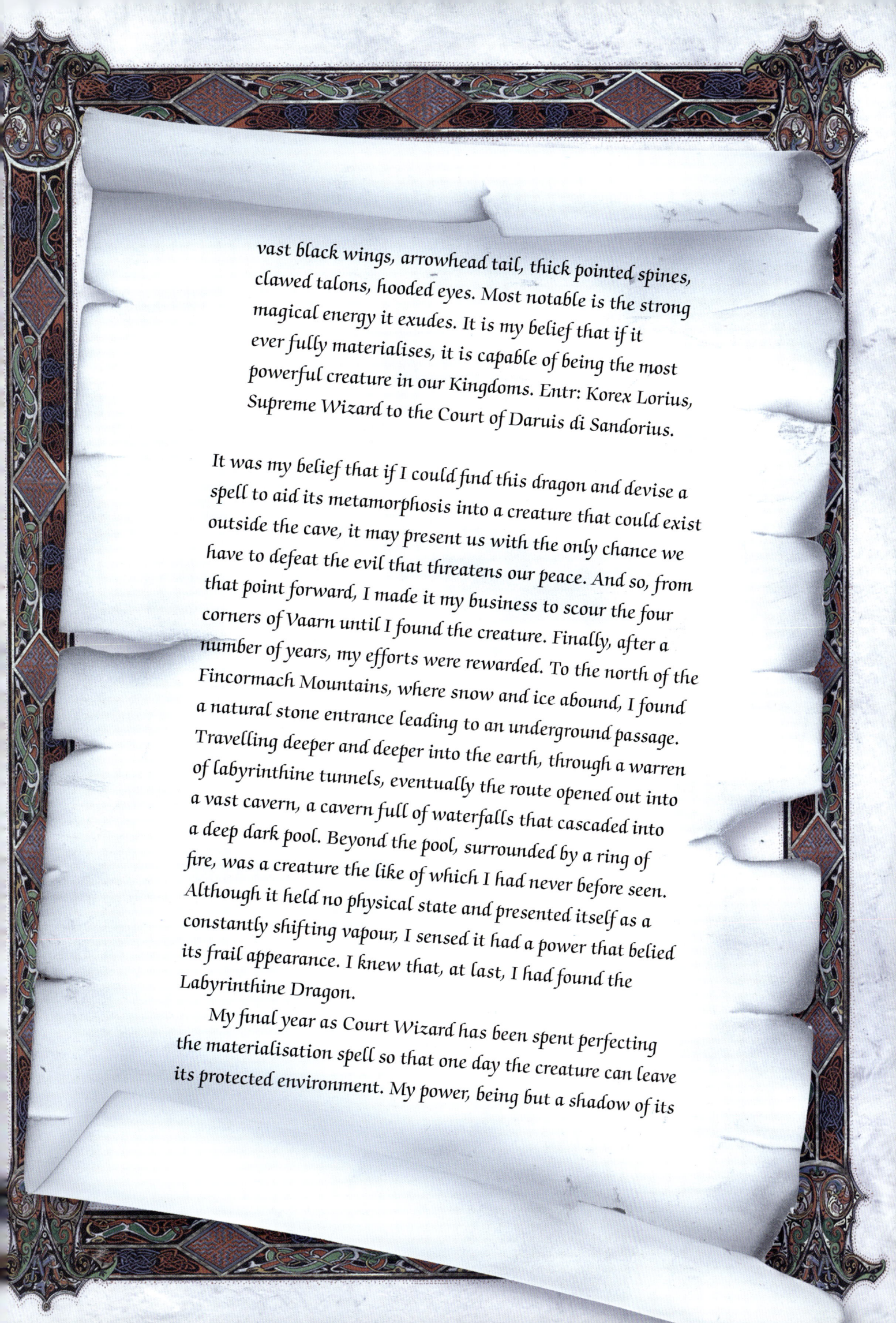

vast black wings, arrowhead tail, thick pointed spines, clawed talons, hooded eyes. Most notable is the strong magical energy it exudes. It is my belief that if it ever fully materialises, it is capable of being the most powerful creature in our Kingdoms. Entr: Korex Lorius, Supreme Wizard to the Court of Daruis di Sandorius.

It was my belief that if I could find this dragon and devise a spell to aid its metamorphosis into a creature that could exist outside the cave, it may present us with the only chance we have to defeat the evil that threatens our peace. And so, from that point forward, I made it my business to scour the four corners of Vaarn until I found the creature. Finally, after a number of years, my efforts were rewarded. To the north of the Fincormach Mountains, where snow and ice abound, I found a natural stone entrance leading to an underground passage. Travelling deeper and deeper into the earth, through a warren of labyrinthine tunnels, eventually the route opened out into a vast cavern, a cavern full of waterfalls that cascaded into a deep dark pool. Beyond the pool, surrounded by a ring of fire, was a creature the like of which I had never before seen. Although it held no physical state and presented itself as a constantly shifting vapour, I sensed it had a power that belied its frail appearance. I knew that, at last, I had found the Labyrinthine Dragon.

My final year as Court Wizard has been spent perfecting the materialisation spell so that one day the creature can leave its protected environment. My power, being but a shadow of its former strength, has not allowed me to release the creature. However, it is my belief that by using the Sankara Amulet as a channel for this spell, any powerful and experienced wizard or sorceress could, with skill, command the dragon. Amaleh, although trained in the art of the spell, as yet has had little experience. This is why I have not, so far, allowed her to perform the magic. This letter is a request for you to release the Amulet for her use when she is more practiced, should the unfortunate circumstances arise that require it. In this way, I may leave with the knowledge that, although I can no longer offer you my protection, I may offer some little hope. I enclose two maps: one revealing the location of the labyrinth; the other, the route through. I also enclose a copy of the spell.

And so my dear Bandred, as you are reading this letter I assume the worst has no doubt occurred. Do not hesitate to put your trust in Amaleh. Over time you will come to know of the powerful gift with which she is bestowed. I have trained her to the best of my ability, and I am sure she will prove a faithful friend.

Yours,

Septimus Angorius

Supreme Wizard
to the Court of Bandred di Sandorius

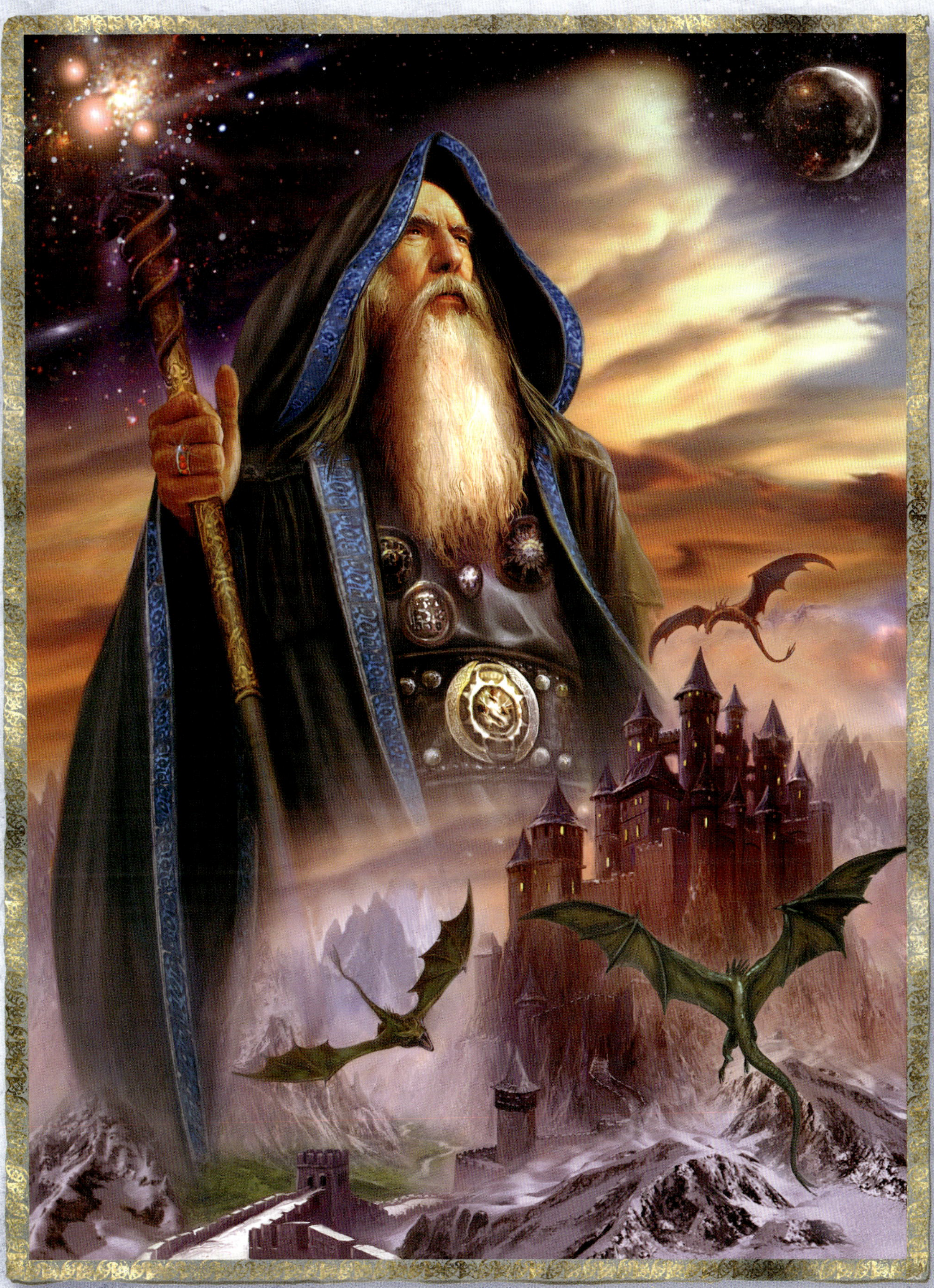

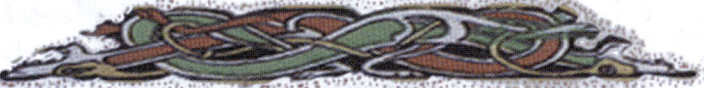

The Wizard Septimus

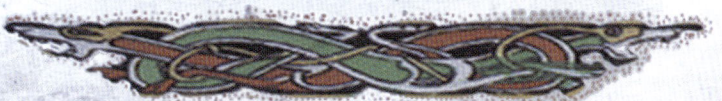

My heart sank. I now understood the full extent of Amaleh's frustration. Septimus' parting gift, which through years of endeavour might now serve to finally stabilise the Kingdoms and banish evil forever, was worthless without the Amulet. Again I felt the heavy weight of responsibility bearing down on me. I needed a plan, but before I had time to consider the letter properly and therefore my options, there was a knock at the door.

'Come,' I called. In stepped Amaleh and seeing the letter in my hand she lifted her head slightly as if to await my response.

'We still have the army with its many experienced and competent soldiers,' I started.

'As you well know, Bandred, they are no match for the evil that has possessed the dragons. Only the lower world knows what magic Count Veldspar has stirred up, but what we are dealing with is no ordinary army. Septimus anticipated this after the last conflict with Ganzicus, which is why he put so much time and effort into finding the Labyrinthine Dragon.'

'But there are things of which you are not aware, Amaleh, we have been developing some powerful weapons in our forge …'

'Don't patronise me, Bandred. Weapons, army … Do you not remember Septimus' struggle?' she roared, her eyes flashing wildly showing her impatience with my defensive attempts.

'So the Labyrinthine Dragon may have given us a better chance,' I argued.

'It is our only chance,' she replied.

'But without the Amulet's power the materialisation is impossible … unless there is something else, some other channel.'

As I spoke my thoughts her expression changed and, regaining her original composure, her eyes engaged with mine once more.

'There is a way, Bandred,' she started slowly. 'When I heard that the Amulet had been stolen, I remembered the Crystal Orb.'

Amaleh raised her arm to reveal the Orb. Set into a silver hilt and made from a single crystal, the ancient ball crackled with energy.

'But the Orb is no match for the Amulet, and you have so little experience,' I argued.

'You have not yet witnessed my true power, Bandred. I am young and gifted, and Septimus has trained me well.'

So, I thought. This was what she had come to say.

'It sounds dangerous,' I said protectively. 'The Amulet provides a channel that surpasses routine magic. What if you fail?'

'My power is strong, Bandred. I will not fail.'

Amaleh was clever. She would get her way. After all it was, as she said, our only chance. However, I needed to let her know it was I who was in command.

'I will think on it. You may go.' And I turned away before my eyes betrayed my voice. As I heard the door gently shut, I summoned my servant.

'Gurin, call a meeting of the High Council at noontide and ask the sorceress, Amaleh, to attend.'

Chapter Three

Under Attack

At noontide I entered the Great Hall where Lord Dedren and the other members of the High Council were waiting. Sitting at the head of the long oak table, I knew I must sound confident in my address and, although they filled my heart with dread, not dwell on the incredible feats that lay ahead. Whatever the future brought, it would not be said that I was not prepared to confront the evil with which we were now faced. In fact, it was Amaleh's confident assertion that she could use the Orb to perform the materialisation spell on the Labyrinthine Dragon that had offered me a way forward. I noticed that she had not yet arrived, but was in no mood to deliberate, so, taking the map and spell from Septimus' letter and spreading them out on the table I revealed the details of the plan.

'And so,' I concluded, 'I will take a small army and accompany Amaleh di Varian on the quest. Once the dragon is in her command, we will be better placed to regain the Sankara Amulet and maintain control of the Four Kingdoms of Vaarn.'

The Council studied the map for some time, warning that the journey to the cave would be particularly arduous, taking in mountains, gorges, valleys, rivers, forests and the notorious Arrias Steppes, and questioning whether we had the capability to tackle the many dragons we would no doubt encounter en route. Despite my own insecurities about the success of the quest, I held a steady voice and dispelled their concerns.

'Lord Dedren, I should like you, supported by the remains of the garrison, to take the role of steward and to defend the palace in my absence.'

When I had finished speaking I looked over in Lord Dedren's direction, expecting his consensus in the matter. Instead his face was dark. He did not speak immediately, but when he did his voice was tight and sharp and lacked its usual warmth.

'Your Highness,' he said, opening with the usual address he adopted for our public discussions, 'perhaps your decision is too hasty. Would it not be more sensible for me to accompany the sorceress Amaleh and for you, our King, to remain a visible presence at the palace – the people need reassurance at this difficult time. May I suggest you reconsider?'

'My mind is set, Lord Dedren,' I responded. Lord Dedren's reaction was surprising.

'Firstly, Your Highness, I should remind you that, as head of state, your responsibility is first and foremost the defence of your people. Cavorting around the Northern Kingdom with a sorceress is hardly a role fit for a king.' He paused and, laughing wryly, looked around the table for support.

'Secondly, your journey to the North will be dangerous. As we know, there are several established dragon territories en route, it will take all the army's strength to overcome them. And finally, without the Amulet you have little chance of controlling this creature of the Labyrinth let alone commanding it to face an army of malevolent dragons. Your plan is flawed. I must insist you reconsider and if not, that the Council take a vote.'

I was surprised at Lord Dedren's uncharacteristic outburst. I had expected him to praise my newfound resolve. I was confused, but decided he was acting protectively. He had known me all my life, had promised my father he would be my guide, it must be difficult to let go now that, at last, I showed signs of taking the lead.

'I am sorry, Lord Dedren,' I said quietly, 'there will be no vote. We leave tomorrow at first light.'

Lord Dedren, who was not used to me, or anyone else for that matter, disagreeing with him shot me a thunderous look, and turning on his heel marched towards the door. But before sweeping out he met Amaleh and, standing aside to let her pass, said, 'It has been decided that our fate lies in your hands, my lady. Let us hope they're as capable as our king believes them to be.'

Nodding at me to acknowledge the approval of this decision, Amaleh introduced herself to the remaining Council members and explained, in her self-assured manner, how she intended to perform the materialisation. Despite their initial apprehensions, they were impressed, and plans to mobilise the army were put in motion. I, a little shaken by Lord Dedren's display, was nonetheless pleased with the outcome of the meeting, finding some relief in the fact that finally a decision had been made.

Later that afternoon, walking along the colonnaded passage that runs between the West and North Towers, I smelt the acrid odour of burnt wood. Out in the courtyard, charred fragments of fallen debris and a scattering of broken stones were slowly being cleared, revealing the gruesome remains of a dragon that had willingly launched itself into a self-destructive attack. When I entered his quarters, my dear brother Alvah was staring out of the window, seemingly mesmerised by the scene below. I joined him, and looking out across the rooftops surveyed the full extent of the damage the palace had sustained.

The sight was pitiful. Most of the wooden outbuildings, homes and workplaces to many of the palace staff, had been destroyed, their ruined half-burned trusses smouldering on the ground. The central courtyard was impassable, buried under a small mountain of rubble where one of the smaller conical towers had collapsed. Here and there battlements had crumbled and were presently a danger to those walking below. But that was not why I had come. Alvah had saved my life and I thanked him.

'It's what I'm trained for,' he said, and then bowing and jesting to mask the embarrassment he felt. 'All in a day's work, my dear brother. I am nothing if not your servant.'

Only a year younger than me, Alvah and I had always been close. For years he had followed me around, that was until I became King and he realised he must forge a life of his own. With his muscular frame and quick and agile movements it was natural for him to train with the garrison. He was well liked and intelligent and, although he had a fiery temper, was always full of fun. It was typical of him, I thought, to make light of so momentous an act. But just as I was considering this, Alvah's expression changed.

'I remember your stories, Bandred, the ones of dragons and spells, of evil and magic and of your adventures with Septimus. They sounded exciting at the time, but …' his voice trailed off and he paused before continuing quietly, '… this was more terrible than I ever could have imagined.' As he spoke, I saw the horror in his eyes and at that moment my determination to fight the evil that threatened our Kingdoms knew no bounds.

First light was bright, the slight mist that rose off the land evaporated as soon as it hit the already warm suntime air. Standing in the lower courtyard I looked up at the palace. There, in its ruinous state and bathed in the sun's glow, it looked almost romantic, raising my spirits for the first time since the attack. The army, gathered outside the Northern Gate and headed by the new military commander Captain Horzan, looked masterful. Rows of soldiers in polished armour held brightly coloured standards that, flapping excitedly in the breeze, seemed to externalise the anticipation of their stalwart bearers below. In stark contrast was the startling appearance of Amaleh. Sitting on her majestic steed, gracefully weaving her way through the noisy crowd, she was clothed from head to foot in white. Gripped in her left hand was the Crystal Orb. I had planned a short speech, and, as I galloped up to take my place next to Captain Horzan, he raised his hand. A hush descended, but before I could utter a word we heard a cry. More cries followed rising to a deafening crescendo and soon my eyes and everyone else's were fixed in the direction of the Jorgas Mountains from where a huge creature came flying towards us.

We could do little but await the beast's arrival. As it flew, its voluminous wings, barely capable of lifting the weight of its colossal body and muscular legs, flapped with a deep slow movement, belying the ferocious speed at which it carried itself. I felt a warm wind that bellowed in gusts, but becoming aware of its stench, soon realised that it was in fact the dragon's hideous breath. At Captain Horzan's command the army dropped to their knees, loaded their crossbows and prepared for the attack. As the creature reached the edge of the forest, the Captain signalled for the release. A hundred bolts whistled through the air, each reaching its target with a dull thud. The creature recoiled and fell to the ground, but, incredibly, regained its posture and blew out its breath in hot fiery blasts. Great balls of flames devoured the landscape and the intense heat sent many people running for cover.

Seeing that the dragon had been badly injured in the first onslaught, and that Captain Horzan had taken shelter from the blast, I shouted for the crossbowmen to regroup and reload. As they did, one of the warriors broke ranks and, with his sword outstretched in front of him, ran full pelt towards the creature, plunging his weapon deep into its leathery belly. What possessed the crazed man I do not know, but during the

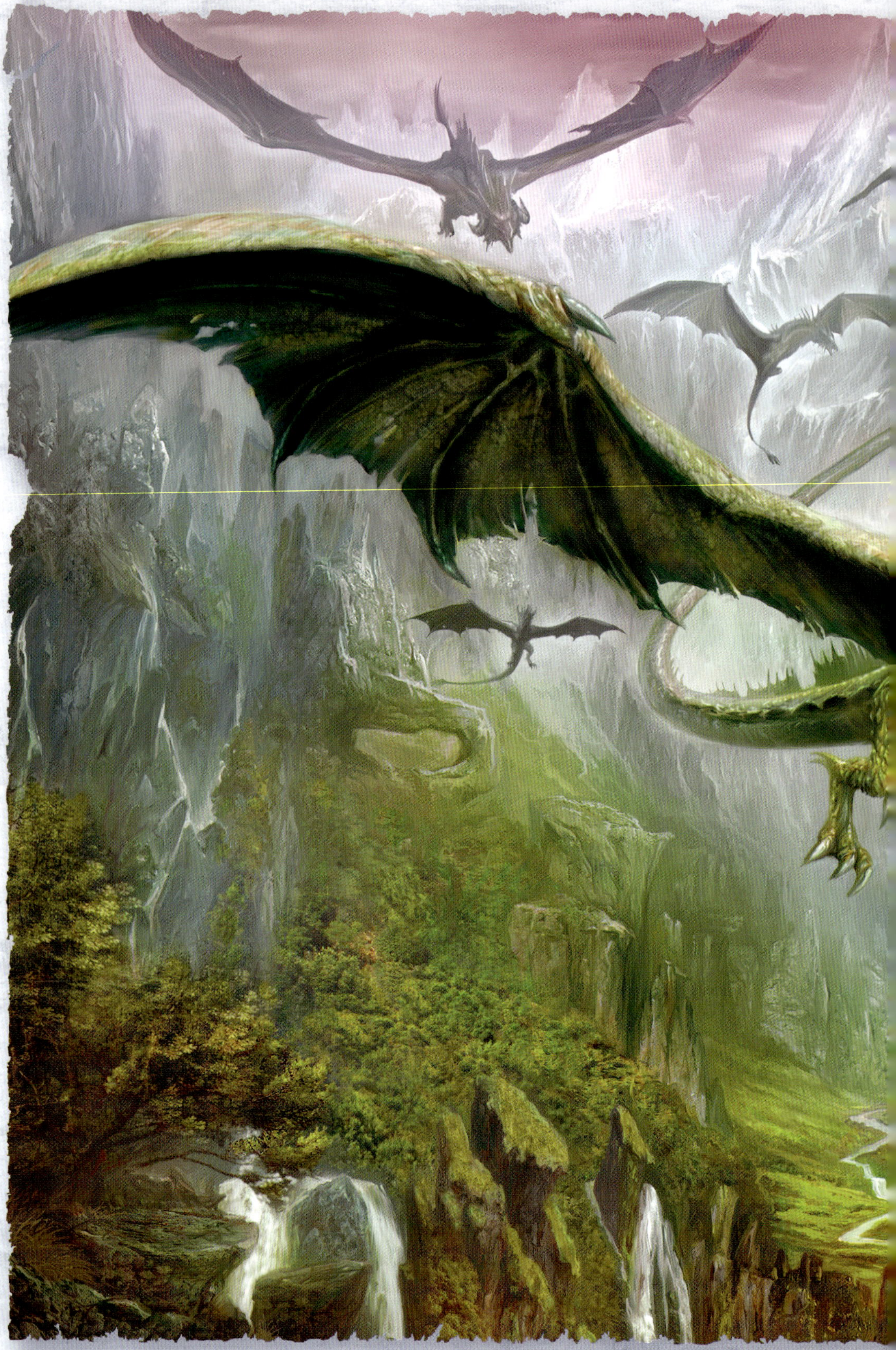

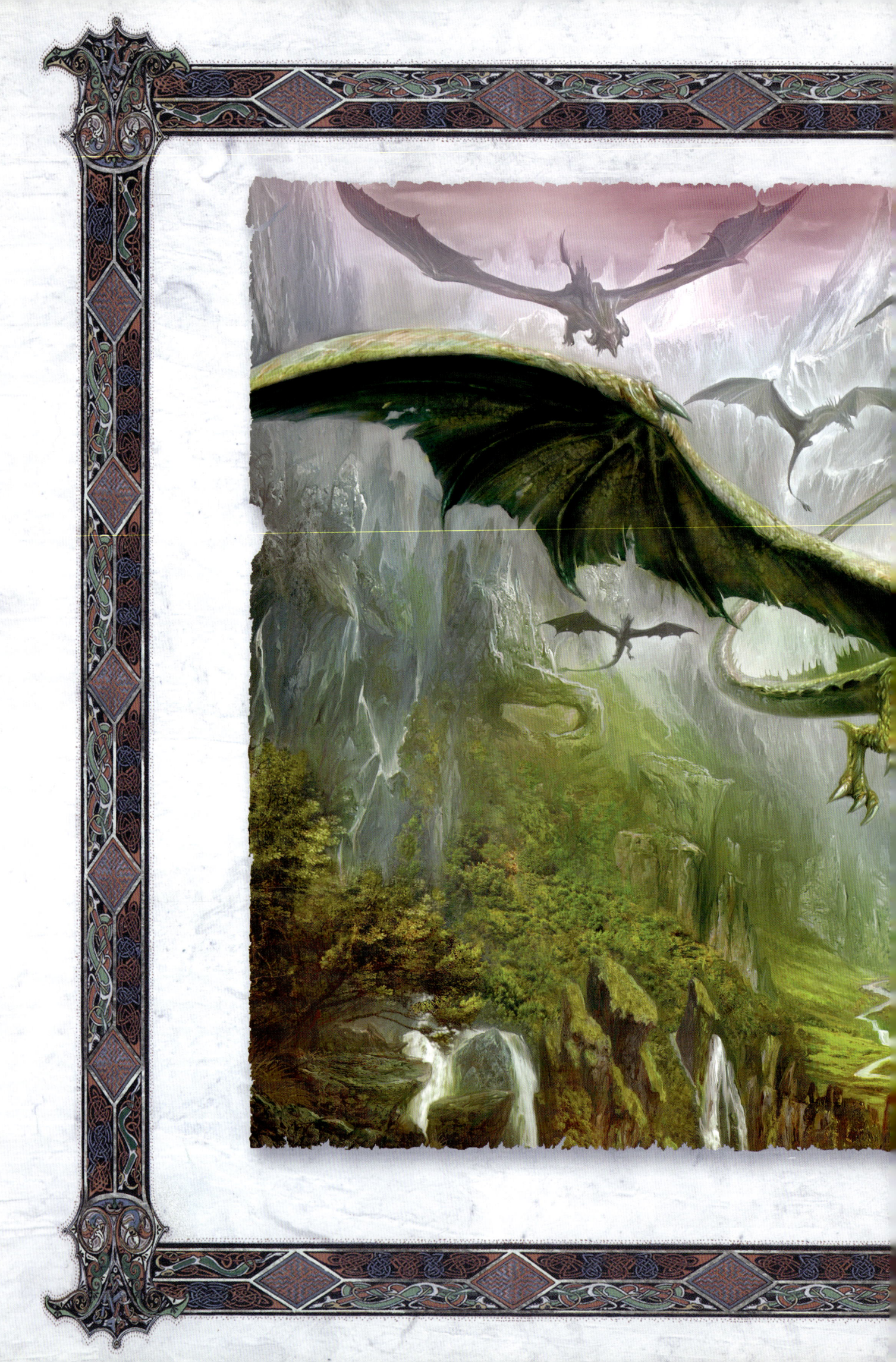

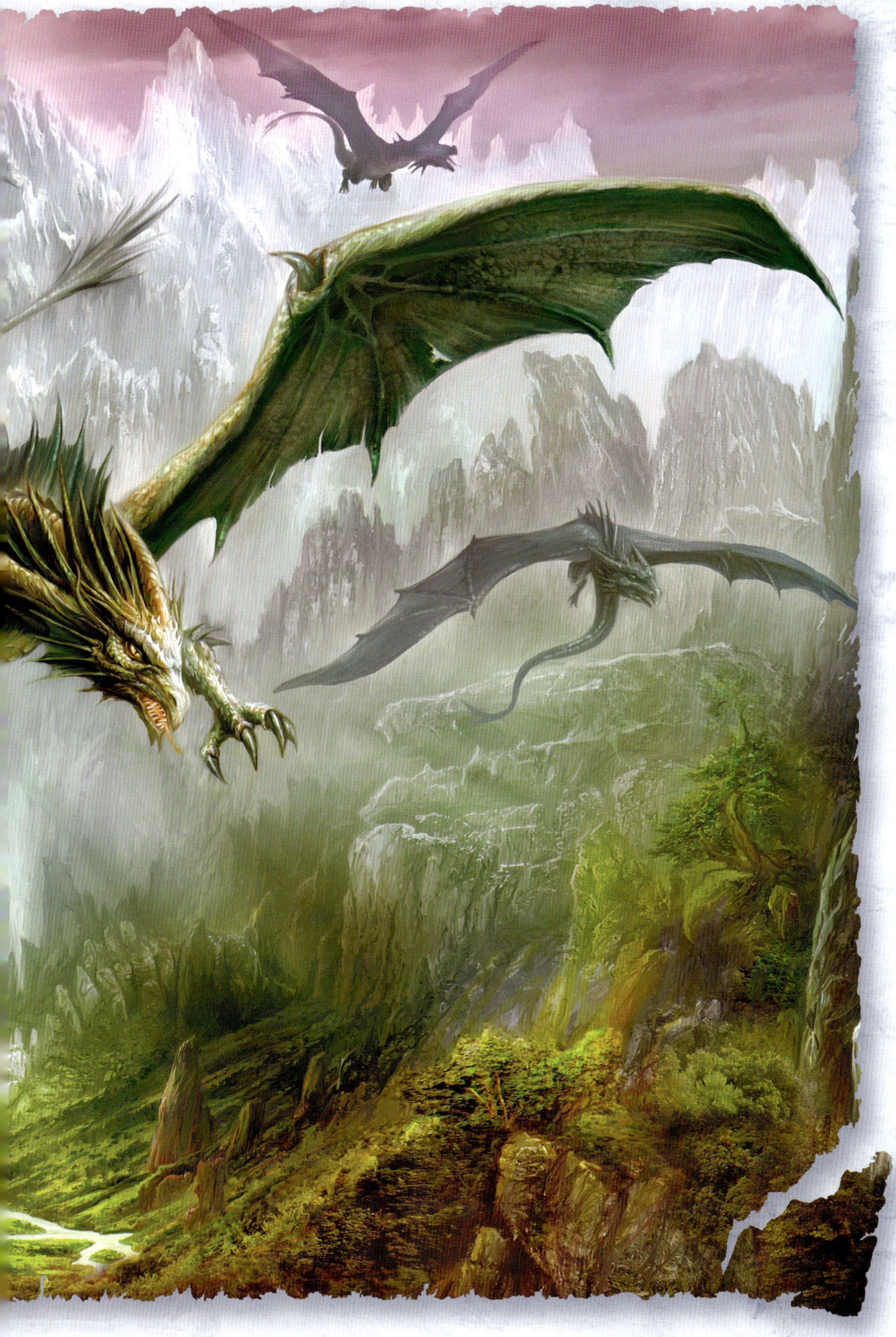

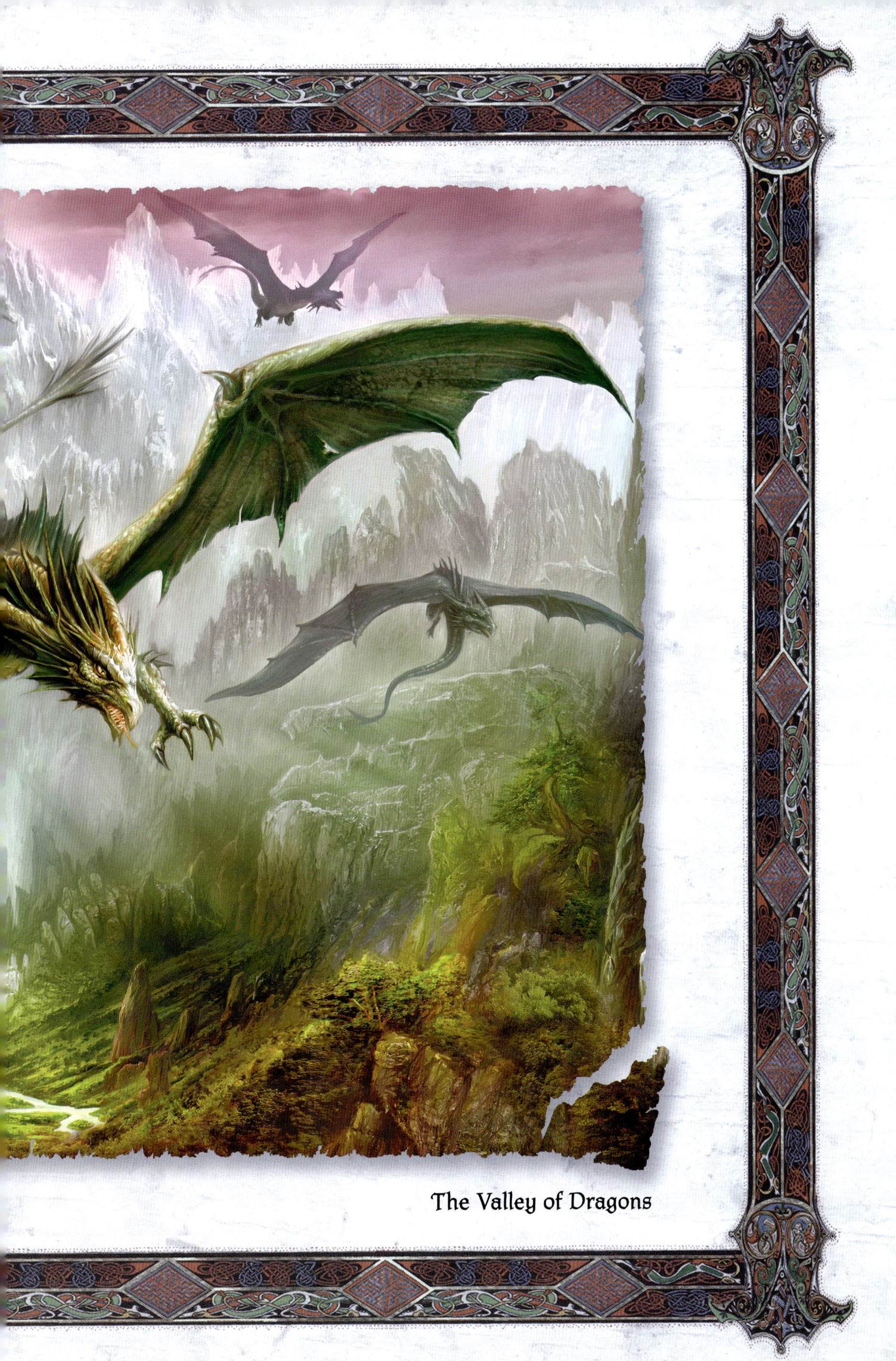

The Valley of Dragons

few seconds he anticipated it would take the dragon to recover, he then brandished his sword wildly above his head, slicing the creature's flesh and piercing the taut skin between the skeletal web of its wings. The beast was growing weak and, during its decline, the warrior made to retreat, allowing clear passage for the second phase of bolts. But before I could signal their release, the dragon once again recovered and, stretching out a giant talon, picked up the valiant warrior, lifted itself from the ground and flew unsteadily away. A few miles off the dragon dropped him. Everyone watched in silence as the solitary figure fell through the air then slipped out of view into the dark forest below.

There was nothing for it but to carry on with the plan. Although no-one on the ground had been killed, there were many injuries. So, faced with the prospect of a depleted army, I had to think fast. Deciding to take with me some of the men from the garrison I was intending to leave with Lord Dedren, I realised the palace was, potentially, a very dangerous place in which to be. Count Veldspar had threatened to return and, with the likelihood of further dragon attacks, I feared more lives would be lost. I had not taken lightly Lord Dedren's words about the responsibility I held towards my people, so I decided to take control. However, what I did next caused so much dissent within the palace household it threatened to overshadow the grave situation we were in. I demanded that those who were able should move out of the palace and into the villages, where I believed they would be less exposed. I expelled all but the courtiers and the garrison from the palace, the place that for many had been their only home.

Of course, they refused. For many it meant leaving behind loved ones; others could see nowhere to go. Thinking they were right, they appealed to the garrison commander to make a stand on their behalf; believing they were wrong, I used force on those who rebelled. And so, unwillingly, they left.

Over the years I have thought long and hard about my decision. What I underestimated, to my subsequent cost, was the strength of their loyalty to the throne: the fact that they saw it as their duty, almost their right, to be allowed to stay and defend their King. If I have learned anything during my long reign, it is that rarely are our actions simply right or wrong, good or evil; the two never exist alone. But back then I thought they did, and so it was that late in the afternoon, wearing my ignorance like a rusty suit of armour, I left the palace and embarked upon the quest.

Chapter Four

Might and Magic

Making our way upstream out of Villiandra along the wide valley floor of the Vielden Pass we soon reached the scrub-covered moors at the foot of the eastern range of the Jorgas Mountains. During these first few days the weather, being clear and bright, did nothing to hamper our progress, and we passed through a number of small towns and villages whose inhabitants offered us provisions and plenty of good cheer as we marched through. Only the bulky dragon-slaying weapons checked our speed. The mood of the men was generally positive. I was pleased to see they exhibited a deep respect for Captain Horzan, who, from time to time, demounted to encourage them in what was a long and tedious march. It had been agreed that I would travel at the front, with the Deputy Commander, Duhra, and that Amaleh would follow behind alongside the Captain. I had spoken little to Amaleh since planning the route before our departure. Using Septimus' map we had decided, for speed rather than ease, to follow the river upstream into the Jorgas Mountains, navigate our way south-east through their range, before travelling further north to traverse the Arrias Steppes towards Andaaja. From there we would plan the final stretch of the journey into the cooler regions of the Northern Territory and the Fincormach Mountains depending on the weather conditions at the time.

The recent attack had been a shock. I had not expected to encounter dragons until we journeyed further abroad. The fact that they were hunting us meant that we all must be extra vigilant. Also, I was full of fear about the days ahead. I had seen Septimus, a wizard potent with power and full of his three-hundred-years experience, struggle desperately with these malevolent creatures. Were Amaleh's abilities such that she stood equal in his role? It had been only a short time since Septimus embarked on 'The Fading', leaving her to serve the realm. She had had little experience without his support. It was my belief that, Amaleh, despite, or perhaps even because of her confidence, would need protection during the journey if our meeting with the Labyrinthine Dragon was to succeed.

And so my thoughts turned to, what I considered, our only real defence. These five heavy weapons, four of which had been specially designed under the instruction of the now-deceased Captain Kronson, commander of the army during the last campaign and veteran dragon slayer, formed our only effective armament against the deadly creatures we were to encounter over the following weeks. The first weapon was a large catapult called *The Winiver* capable of throwing up to 10 weights of projectile using the tension from a twisted cord. Extremely accurate and relatively easy to manoeuvre, its main advantage was that we did not have to transport its missiles, which could be found in the form of large rocks. The second weapon, *The Talija*, was mounted on a platform. Consisting of a cleverly designed shooting wheel perpendicular to its supporting wooden frame, it could be loaded with spiked balls enabling a continuous launch of vicious projectiles. Whilst useful as a deterrent, it was unlikely that this weapon would be capable of destroying its target. *The Mazool*, although hand held, was extremely powerful, a fully enclosed missile sheath allowing its bronze-tipped weapons to be coated in deadly poison. Quick to set up and load, it was expected to prove the most effective tool for killing. The forth weapon, named *The Kronson*, was another catapult, this one firing a huge square of fine but strong metal mesh. Although not designed to kill, it might well disable a creature for long enough for any of the other weapons to be loaded. We had also brought along *The Madagan Crossbow*, a weapon that had more than proved its worth when it was used many years ago to kill the leviathan Beast of Gramarnica.

On the fourth day we began meandering our way up the steep-sided valley along a series of rising paths. At first our climb was barely perceptible, the view shielded by the many tall evergreens that clothed the fertile slopes. However, as we broke out of the woodland, the rapidity of our ascent soon became apparent. Looking down into the valley below, my eyes followed the river as it broadened and emptied into the glistening Pharamond Sea. To the west, rising up from the land, were the jagged peaks of the Jorgas Mountains, in front, to the north, an impossibly high ridge, which widened out to form the plateau that was to be our destination that day.

Reflecting on the unspoiled beauty our Kingdoms afforded, I could not help but compare it to Svaal. Although I had never visited, recent reports told of a place of pitiful desolation. But it had not always been that way. As a boy, my father had accompanied his father to Svaal on a number of state visits. Then it formed part of the Northern Territory, and they were honoured guests of Count Veldspar's father, who although kindly was ultimately weak. My father talked of a hospitable place, where people enjoyed life but worked hard in the many towns and villages scattered throughout this cold mountainous region. But the elderly Count Veldspar was no match for his son. When the young Veldspar started dabbling in the evil arts, his malevolent ambitions came to the fore, launching him on a ceaseless crusade to win for Svaal its independence. As his father's health failed, Veldspar took over, defending the borders with his dark magic so that no interference from the Kingdoms was possible without devastating loss. Eventually, during my father's reign, an agreement was drawn up to recognise Svaal's independence. That was the beginning of its demise. Now under military rule, its people had to live with famine through lost crops and disease, and endure its ruined towns and cities.

Shivering, the air felt considerably cooler here and as we travelled higher and higher up the winding rocky path, a light dusting of snow began to creep in underfoot. After a while the troops guiding and pulling the huge weapons grew weary and when the path opened up to reveal a lake, it seemed as good a spot as any to take a rest. Most of the soldiers dropped their weary limbs onto the ground and drank from their flasks, some lay on their backs taking the opportunity for a short nap, whilst others checked their equipment. The more energetic, in high spirits, were mock fighting and generally horsing around.

Captain Horzan spotted it first: the rippling of the lake. This in itself would not have been unusual, but he had noticed that even at this altitude there was no breeze. Suddenly and with a violent force the calm waters were shattered. A hideous creature, its jaws brimming with pointed teeth, a viscous substance dripping from its gills, leapt upwards and out of the water, the huge muscular coils of its snake-like body following as it landed on the far side of the lake. Then, with a swift slithering action it was upon us, and, seizing a warrior in its fat trunk, bent its head to attack. Within moments a number of soldiers had set upon it, forcing their blades in between its scales and piercing its leathery skin.

There was no time to load the larger weapons, so grasping *The Mazool* I looked around for somewhere from which to take my aim. Climbing onto a rocky ledge, I found my position and quickly loaded the arrow. With the release, I cursed. Such was the creature's activity – it was reeling from left to right – I knew the arrow would miss its mark. Loading the second, I could see we were running out of time. The creature was using its tail as a club, launching its assailants out of the way, and, at the same time, still holding its wriggling captive firm. In shooting the arrow a little to the left, I anticipated the beast's movements. The arrow struck, and within moments the noxious poison had worked its magic. With a resounding thud the creature collapsed, releasing its prisoner with such force he was thrown high into the air before landing awkwardly on the ground.

It was to everyone's surprise that, despite so startling and frenzied

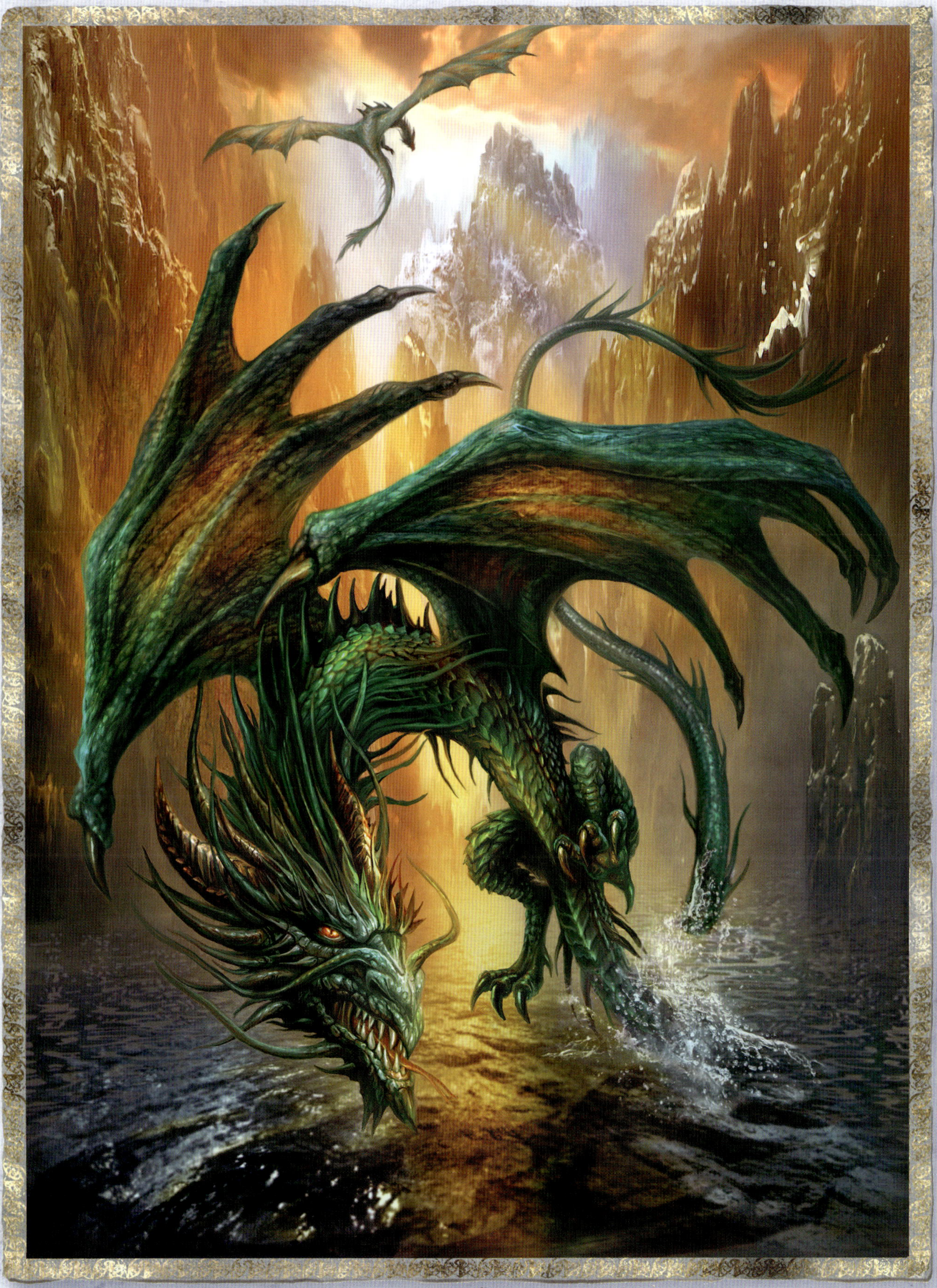

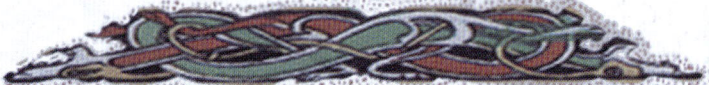

Dragon of the Lake

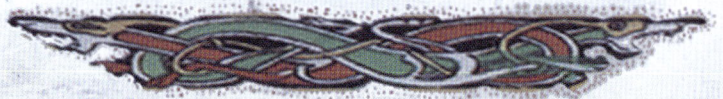

an attack, no-one had sustained a serious injury. The poor soul who had been squeezed half to death was much revived after consuming a tonic administered by Amaleh, and although, like many of the men, his body was badly bruised, there seemed to be no permanent damage. Not wishing to leave the ominous creature to attract scavengers, I ordered the soldiers to throw its carcass back into the lake. With considerable effort they heaved it towards the bank and gently started to feed its vast trunk into the water. After a while the weight of the creature pulled it forwards and, gaining speed, it seemed to take on a life of its own and quickly slithered out of sight.

Although I felt some sense of accomplishment at having killed my first beast, this terrifying interlude had caught us off guard and it was with increasing trepidation that we travelled onwards. Continuing along the ever-steepening path towards the ridge, I took the opportunity to ride back to Captain Horzan and Amaleh. The Captain smiled warmly, congratulating me on my fast reactions and for preventing what could have been a fatal attack. But it was not his comments I most desired. As I glanced at Amaleh, I noticed she was not smiling so I asked playfully, 'Do you not wish to commend my dragon-slaying skills too, Amaleh?'

'It is nothing less than I would expect,' she replied.

'Ah, I can see you set your standards high. What would you have me do?'

'In the face of pure evil, that beast was a maiden. Slay a real dragon and ask me then.'

Her rebuke humiliated me and, kicking my heels hard into my horse, I galloped back to Deputy Commander Duhra to nurse my ruined pride. I continued the rest of the journey in silence, meditating on a growing determination to prove myself worthy of my title.

Eventually we reached the grassy plateau and pitched camp close to a broad overhang overlooking a deep ravine. Weary from our day's adventure and in much need of sleep, we consumed some swiftly prepared food and settled down for the night even before the last of the light had disappeared from the sky.

We were woken by the watchman's cries followed shortly by a cacophonous roar that echoed throughout the gorge. Running to the edge of the precipice and looking downwards into the abyss, I saw nothing at first. But then, preceded by a blast of air containing the unmistakable reek of dragon's breath, the beast appeared out of the gloom. The dragon was a grotesque vision. All razor-sharp teeth and shiny black talons, its leathery vein-crossed wings raised it higher and higher as it flew past our camp and perched on a plateau some way off. I knew that dragons have a truly phenomenal sense of sight and because of this often attack at night, so was well aware it had the advantage over us. With little time to lose, I quickly found Captain Horzan and we discussed which of the weapons to ready. Whilst deciding, however, I had noticed Amaleh making her way down a path towards a rocky outcrop. Concerned for her safety, I followed, hoping to intercept her path, but at that moment the creature returned billowing huge plumes of fire and smoke across our camp and surveying the area with its gleaming eyes.

When the smoke cleared the dragon had disappeared from sight. Amaleh, having reached her destination, held the Crystal Orb low in her outstretched arms and started to turn in slow circles. I saw her lips moving as she cast her spell. Gradually, the rocky floor beneath her feet took on the appearance of a series of ever-decreasing concentric circles overlaid with two pentangles — the sign of the sorceress. Round and round she danced, slowly raising the glowing Orb. As she did, the air was filled with a protective dome that glimmered from time to time against the inky backdrop each time it caught the soft light. I froze, entranced by the elegance and beauty of so simple but powerful an act and at the same time paralysed in fear for her safety.

The dragon returned and, this time, having identified its target, blew a huge ball of fire in Amaleh's direction. Fortunately the dome was strong and held the flames at bay. Then the dragon let forth another deadly spit. Again the dome worked its magic, but it had served its purpose and I knew what was coming. Watching with apprehension, Amaleh waited calmly until the dragon took its next breath, then swiftly, lowering the shield, she raised the Orb high into the air and chanted a few powerful words. This time the Orb glowed brightly and a stream of white fire cracked through the air towards the beast, striking its mouth and killing it instantly.

We watched in anticipation as the dragon fell, tumbling through the air, its body torn to tatters as time and time again it crashed into the mountain wall. All the while it screeched, a resounding cacophony that echoed in our ears. When at last the noise stopped, I looked towards Amaleh. She was lying motionless on the floor. Full of dread, I ran down to her seemingly lifeless body, but just as I got there she recovered. Holding me back with her eyes, I quickly slowed down.

There was little point in returning to our tents that night so the men packed up. I noticed they treated Amaleh with extreme reverence, even offering to carry her tent for her, and couldn't help but feel a little envious. I had a long way to go to command such respect from my people.

We had reached the highest point of our journey and so, as day broke we started our descent, travelling in wide zigzag movements down the mountainside. Despite the dangers ahead, I enjoyed our morning's effort and by evening we had reached the edge of the Traillian Forest, a vast area of woodland that blocked our path to the Arrias Steppes.

That evening, after we had set up camp, I took the opportunity to visit Amaleh in her tent. She had not consulted anyone before embarking on her dangerous defence and, although I had to admire her skill, it would be wrong of me to allow her independence to go unchecked. Whenever we met, however, she always seemed to get the better of me so this time I was determined to think carefully before I spoke. I found her pouring over 'The Book of Serafan'.

'Spells for killing dragons?' I inquired amiably.

'What do you want, Bandred?'

Immediately feeling angry, I found it infuriating how she could so easily shift my mood.

'I wanted to remind you of your position, Amaleh,' I responded. 'As Court Sorceress you are in my service and should have sought my agreement before deciding to use your magic to destroy the dragon.'

'Agreement, Bandred? If I had waited for your agreement, we all could have died. It was no time for indecision.' She turned back to her book and when I didn't leave added, 'Was there anything else?'

Keeping calm, I decided to try a different tack.

'You need to conserve your power, Amaleh. Having witnessed Septimus' demise during the last campaign, I am concerned for your safety. You will need considerable strength when you meet the Labyrinthine Dragon. Do not weaken yourself unnecessarily before then.'

'I am touched by your concern Bandred, but you needn't worry. For some time I have known that I have 'The Gift'. Septimus, on the other hand, had merely 'The Calling'. I have the potential to be twice the magi he was, if only I were allowed to prove it.'

She had revealed her vulnerability. For all her harsh words, Amaleh was desperate to put her power to the test. And so, despite her arrogance, my mood softened and I replied, 'You will, Amaleh. In time, you will.'

Chapter Five

Darkness and Light

I had been warned that the next stage of our journey would be challenging. The Arrias Steppes is a vast region of lowlands with a varied landscape. Travelling from west to east, the plain initially yields field upon field of calf-length grass, which, although harmless in itself, had been reported by previous travellers to give rise to huge suffocating clouds of pollen and insects, making progress interminably slow. I knew that eventually, the swathes of rain due to arrive from the mountain ranges beyond Andaaja, would cause the climate to become damper and the dry fields would give way to the central boggy tracts. Finally, when we approached the Fincormach Mountains and entered the Northern Territory, it would turn bitterly cold — weather we could ill-afford at the end of what would undoubtedly prove to be an exhausting journey. Furthermore, the whole region was largely uninhabited, so there were no towns or villages in which we would be able to take respite.

I had estimated that to traverse the Steppes would take a full ten days, after which the plan was to recuperate for some much needed rest at Andaaja Castle, home to Lord Rulan, one of my father's oldest and dearest friends. It was some years since I had seen the man, but my memories of him were fond. Charming and entertaining, it was the thought of him and his ever-welcoming hospitality that kept me going through the most fearful moments of those following days.

However, before we could tackle the Arrias Steppes, we had to make our way through the forest. Amaleh and I had decided that, rather than losing time travelling around the woodland, it would make more sense to follow a direct route. We set off at a pace, but quickly realised that navigating through would prove more difficult than anticipated. Tall broad-leaved trees that stretched their branches into the clouds grew so dense that they shut out the sun, leaving us dark and dank on the ground. So we split up and travelled in small groups, each taking turns at the lead.

After a number of hours, we became aware of terrible caterwauls: piercing screeches the like of which I had never heard before. Captain Horzan ordered the men to ready their weapons but continue advancing in groups. Onwards we weaved, through the maze of trees, towards the shouts of those leading, all the while listening to the directionless screams that seemed to be closing in around our troop. I smelled fear in the air, and when the shouts turned to cries, expected the worst.

Suddenly, a swarm of dragons — all clammy wings and high-pitched screams — hovered above us. They had olive scales, leathery wings and talons like sharpened graphite. I reached for my sword and slashed the air in huge arcs above my head. The men in my group were doing the same. Then one, holding his throat, fell to his knees, and I noticed that his eyes and nose were trickling with blood, as if some vile poison had entered his body. But the creatures had not touched us. I realised at once that they must have been emitting some lethal vapour. Running over to the man I could see he was already dead, his pallid face streaked with rivulets of his own blood.

Quickly, I covered my nose and mouth with a cloth and signalled for the others to do the same. Aware that the rest of the troops were innocent prey and must be warned, I shouted loudly into the deadening air. We ran, dodging tree trunks, all the time being hunted by the terrible squawking swarm. The forest was too dark to see our assailants, but the haunting cries of those being attacked by the venomous beasts rang loudly in our ears. After a while the trees became our friends and eventually, unable to keep sight of us, the creatures fell behind. Still onwards we ran — our legs numb through exertion, our chests bursting with pain and our dry mouths drinking in great gulps of air. Gradually the trees began to thin out, their bushy canopies no longer touching until eventually the path became clear. Finally free, we flung ourselves to the ground, exhausted and terrified by the horrific ambush.

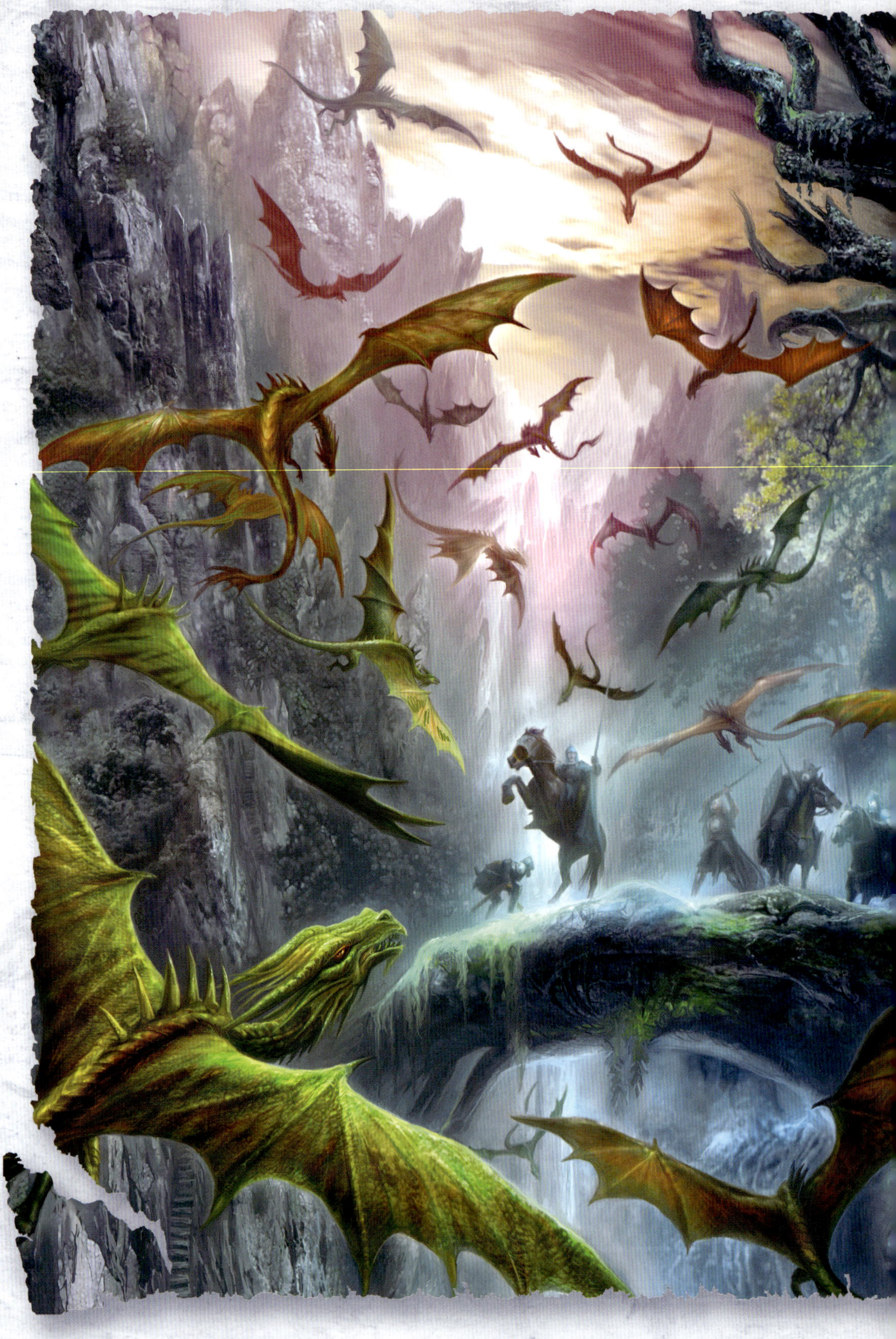

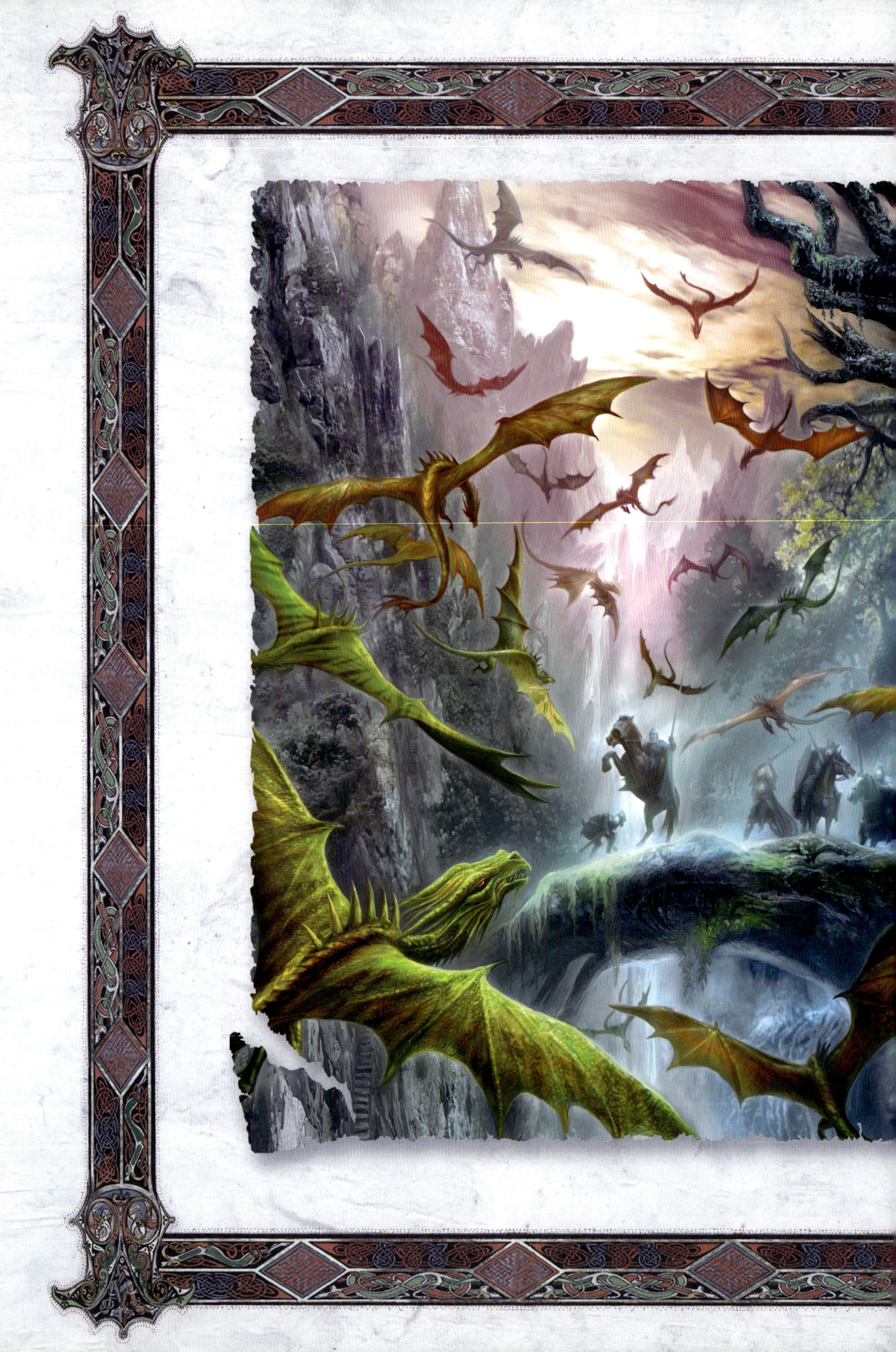

The Forest Swarm

As group by group the men found their way out of the forest, it was clear we had taken heavy casualties. Nine men were missing and *The Talija* had been abandoned. After some thought and with inevitable regret, I decided the forest was too dangerous to re-enter. We would have to leave the unburied bodies to rot. But that was not all that concerned me. Some of the men were complaining that painful blisters had appeared on their bodies. This was most unusual and even the physician was at a loss to know what had caused the infections. Amaleh administered a lotion to each of the sufferers, which went a little way to relieving their discomfort. The creatures, it seemed, were particularly deadly and I wondered whether Count Veldspar had already started to use the Amulet's power to spread his evil throughout the land. Urging the men onwards, I was more determined than ever to make a success of the seemingly impossible tasks ahead.

Having witnessed the depth of evil that was unleashed by Ganzicus many years ago, I knew at least part of what we were up against. But the fact that Count Veldspar also had access to the Amulet's higher power made the prospect far more terrible. I was well aware that this, coupled with the fact that the Amulet was one of the Kingdoms' most important symbols of power, made it a most desirable possession. However, something puzzled me, and during the hours of laborious journeying, I kept turning the question around in my mind. How did Count Veldspar know where to find the Amulet? On the day of the attack there was no searching, he went straight to the vaults in which it was held. Only a few members of the High Council, Alvah and Amaleh knew of its whereabouts. It is possible the Count used a visionary device, but as I understood it, the Amulet could protect itself against this. I knew I could trust my brother implicitly, and the members of the Council were all faithful men. Amaleh, as Court Sorceress, should be beyond suspicion. So the question remained unanswered.

On the eighth day, as we moved further north out of the central region of the Steppes towards the Fincormach Mountains, the weather grew noticeably cooler. Soon it became chillingly cold. The air stung our faces and we were forced to put on our bulky overmantles. Andaaja Castle was situated facing west in an elevated position just above a narrow canyon on the east side of the mountains. I had issued word of our plans before the journey began, but had not heard word from Lord Rulan since and was slightly anxious about whether he would be expecting us. Towards the end of the afternoon, Captain Horzan sent a scout to inform him of our forthcoming arrival. I was concerned for the welfare of the sick men, and everyone in the troop was in need of proper sustenance and rest.

We were in sight of the castle when the Captain, who had taken the lead, halted the troop. I rode up to find out why. What I saw could only be described as horrific: the bloody, headless and limbless trunk of the scout lay pitifully on the ground, his savaged skin and smashed bones parting to reveal his innermost organs. It was a depraving sight; one that I am sure made each man swear to avenge. Some turned their heads, doubling their bodies as they retched; others openly wept; a few disengaged their emotions, the only indication of this being a cold hard gaze.

I looked to the mountains. It was probable that the beast that had carried out this violent attack came from somewhere within. If so, he would, no doubt, return. Calculating that if we moved forward without challenging the creature, we risked a surprise attack later on, I decided we should try and lure the beast back. Moving the troop into a sheltered position underneath the overhang of a cliff, I ordered the men to ready their hand weapons and *The Winiver*. Then, taking the horn from my saddle and blowing it with all my breath, I rode out into the middle of the canyon towards the site of the attack. Its low note echoed loudly. There was nothing to do but wait.

Soon enough we saw the creature emerge flapping its vast wings in dramatic arcs that met first above, then below its body. Its liquid eyes scanned the area for movement, and catching sight of me, let out a piercing scream. Here I took my cue, and cantering full pelt towards the overhang, I prayed the weapons would provide the back up I required. But the creature was faster than I had anticipated and, swooping down, it let forth a long tongue of flame. Feeling its heat on my back, I raced away, praying that *The Winiver* was ready to launch, its bundle tightly wound and a large boulder in its cup. However, although *The Winiver*'s range was further than most catapults, the dragon was still not close enough. I didn't know how much longer my horse could carry me at speed, and visions of the scout's dismembered body flashed in front of my eyes. Finally, *The Winiver*'s arm was unleashed and its huge projectile shot over my head. A dull thud, ensuing scream and following cheer from the troops confirmed to me that the missile had hit its mark and, allowing myself a glimpse backwards, I saw the creature had received a blow to its breast, a gaping hole indicating damage to its scaly outer armour and revealing its flesh. Still it flew. For a while the beast circled, not daring to come closer, but I knew it would return. When finally I reached the overhang, I seized *The Madagan Crossbow*. I had seen how effective this weapon was when Septimus used it against the mighty Beast of Gramarnica, surely it would serve me well, too.

Gradually, the dragon recovered and, incensed by our success, made several low swoops, showering us with shafts of fire and crashing into the overhang, disengaging a number of large shards that fell onto the soldiers below. I could see the situation was deteriorating and our only chance at defeat was an arrow. The creature once again flew up into the sky, using the mountain thermal to provide its lift. I aimed the bow upwards and waited for its return, then, as soon as it began its descent, I unleashed the arrow. The machine recoiled and as I was thrown backwards onto the ground, I watched the powerful lance rushing towards its target, whilst all the time its target hurtled towards us. Such was the speed of the arrow, the dragon spotted it too late, and with a resounding thump, it plunged deep into the beast's underbelly.

The dragon's scream was all that could be heard as it reeled from the impact before falling and landing with a deafening crash on the ground. With a final breath, the dragon's tail twitched and its body slumped onto the earth. A loud cheer went up and everyone rushed towards it in high spirits, the tension of the last few minutes having been very much relieved.

Exhausted but encouraged by our successful attack, we made our way to the castle portal where our host met us. Lord Rulan had watched the events with anticipation, and then relief, and was at the ready with a staff of kind and caring servants who helped us up the steep-tunnelled walk to his cheerful abode. As we were being shown to our rooms, I glanced at Amaleh, hoping to receive some small acknowledgement of my achievement that day. My optimism was rewarded when, catching my eye, I saw a half-smile spread slowly across her lips.

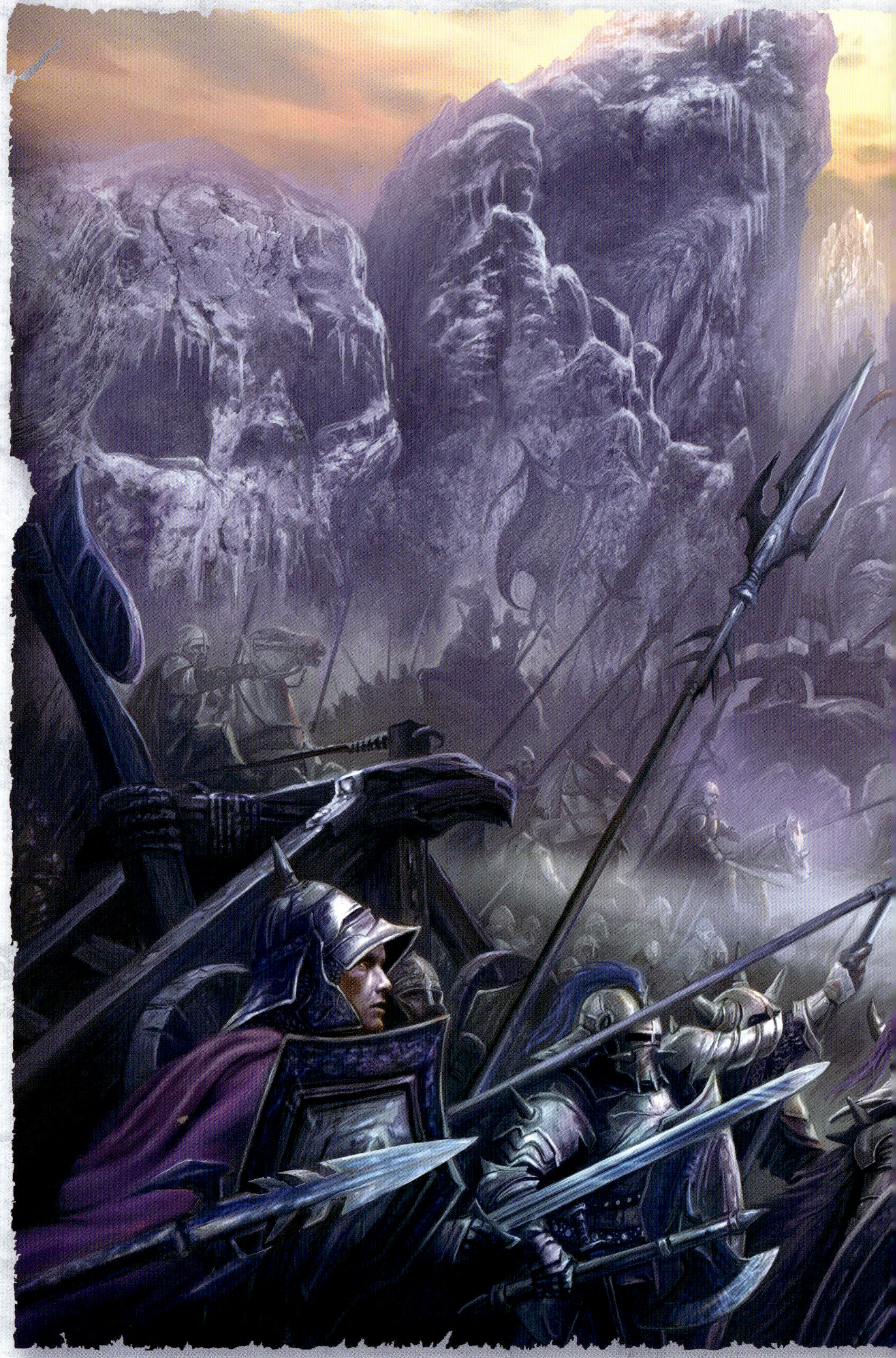

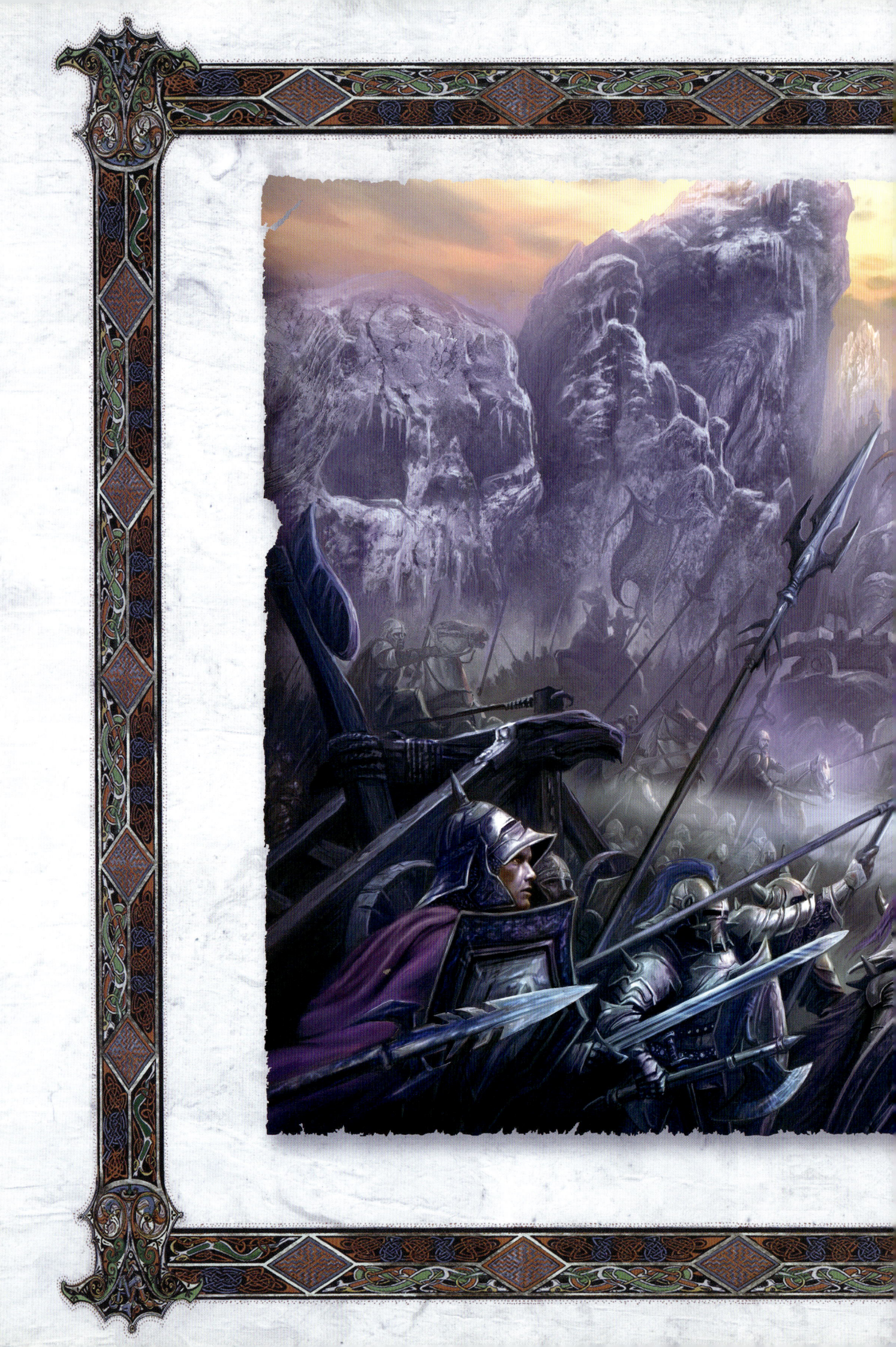

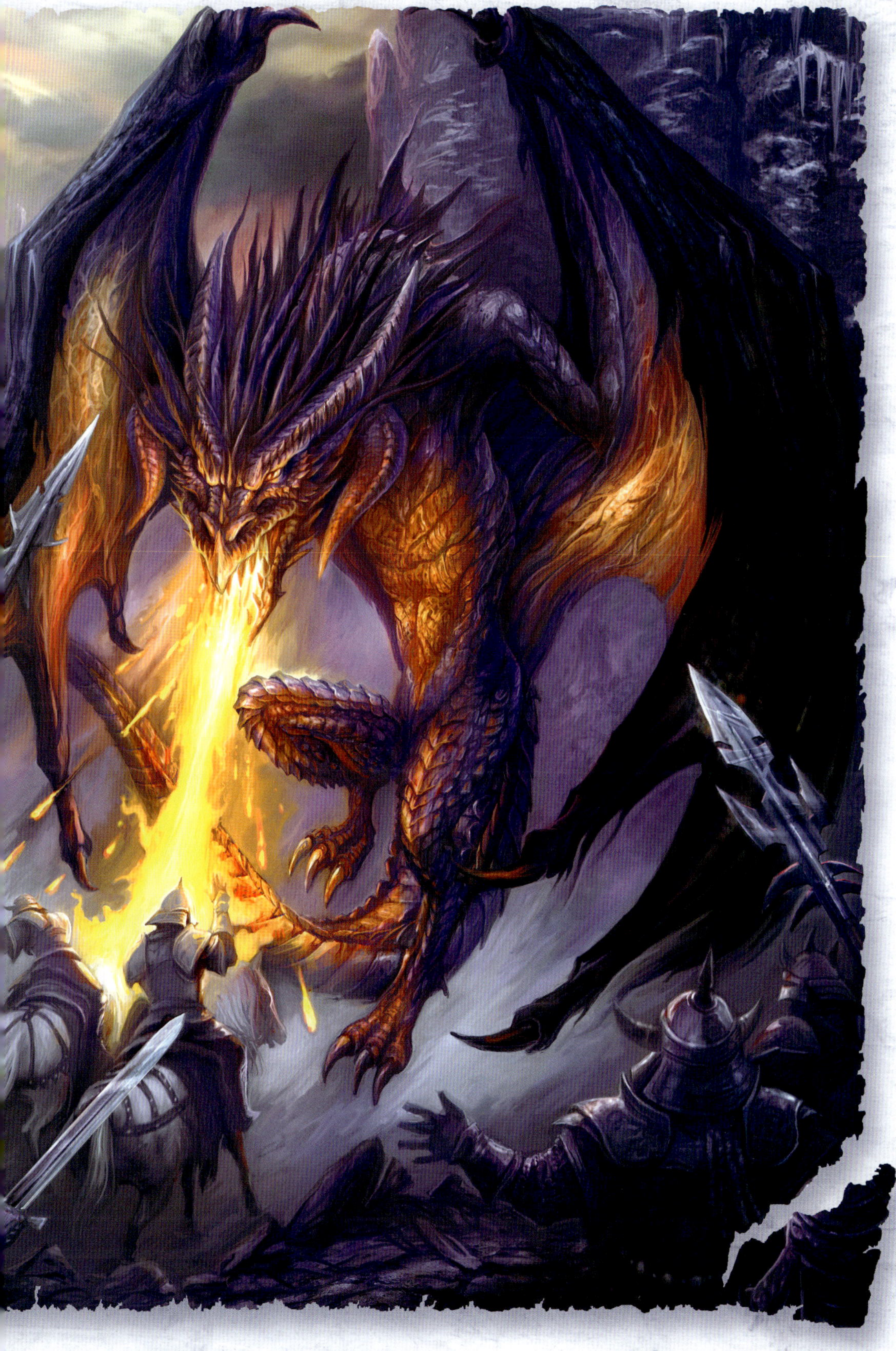

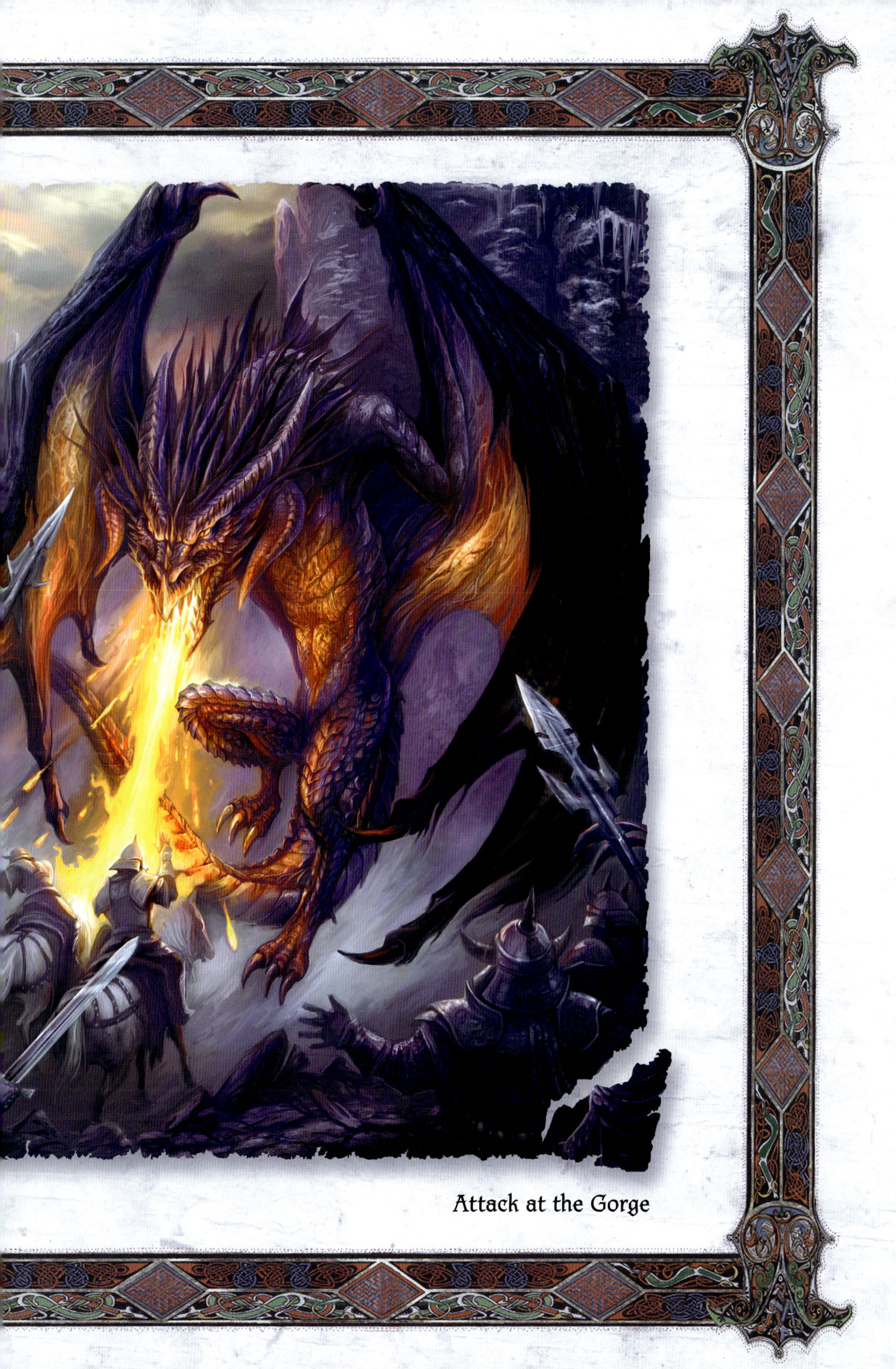

Attack at the Gorge

Chapter Six

Trapped

By nightfall we were all gathered in the magnificent Great Hall of Andaaja Castle. From the dark and draughty place in which we had congregated upon our arrival, it had been transformed. Candlelight lifted it out of its gloom, richly-coloured tapestries adorned the walls and in the central hearth, a warming fire burned. Jugs of ale had been set upon the tables, and needless to say, it was not long before the men had settled down, alongside the company of the castle, to the serious business of merriment. Lord Rulan, by my side at the high table, was entertaining me with genial tales of his younger years, many of which featured my father. He was a passionate man – larger than life but perceptive with it – I could see why my father had enjoyed his company. After a while, Lord Rulan stood to deliver his welcome speech and I drifted off, thinking about earlier in the evening when, in his private chambers, he had asked me what assistance he might offer. Suddenly, I had felt exhausted.

'There are a few practicalities, such as extending your hospitality to allow the sick men time to recuperate, that would help ease my mind. However, it is your thoughts I most desire. You knew my father. He was a good and kind man who ruled the Four Kingdoms successfully for many years. He made the right decisions and gained the respect of his people. What is it that he possessed that I do not?'

'The Amulet for starters,' jested Lord Rulan. I managed a weak smile.

'Oh, Bandred, I am an old man, what do I know about the qualities of kingship? But one thing I can say is that I recognise in you the struggles your father experienced in his younger years. Kingship did not always sit comfortably on his shoulders and never more so than when the young and eager Lord Dedren was snapping at his heels.'

'What do you mean? Lord Dedren always supported my father.'

'In your lifetime, maybe, but when they were young, Lord Dedren was impatient with your father. He felt he would have made a better king. After a while his impatience revealed itself as jealousy and the brothers had a falling out. It was your father who, in my opinion, feeling guilty at the very thing he could never change – the fact that he was the first-born son and heir to the throne, reached out to repair the relationship. He committed to seek Lord Dedren's council in every matter, pandering to his brother's egotistical nature.'

'Which would explain why Lord Dedren was so furious when I made a decision without consulting him,' I mused.

'You will find your way, Bandred,' Lord Rulan said, 'Your display of bravery earlier this afternoon was impressive. It will not have gone unnoticed by those you lead. Come, let us to the Great Hall and, for one evening at least, may you leave your troubles behind.'

I snapped out of my reverie as a loud cheer went up. Lord Rulan let the noise continue for a while, then held up his hand, signalling for quiet. A hush descended.

'And now let us pay tribute to our brave king, leader of this noble quest.' With Lord Rulan's words, everyone stood.

'To King Bandred,' they hailed, raising their cups, to which Lord Rulan replied. 'Let the banquet begin.'

Suddenly the hall became a flurry of activity. Servants bore trays laden with the most exquisite delicacies, the men, once again, helped themselves to the jugs of ale and all the while minstrels sang songs that honoured our victory over the Dragon of Fincormach. The atmosphere in this castle exuded warmth and joviality. This was such a contrast to the many days of hard travelling we had endured, it seemed to me almost unreal. And so I decided to heed Lord Rulan's advice and give myself up to the respite offered and the labours that lay ahead.

'What would you have, King Bandred?' asked Lord Rulan, turning to fill my cup. 'Let my servants fetch for you what you will.'

'Your hospitality is most welcoming, Lord Rulan,' I replied, 'But please, treat me as you would any man here, I deserve no more.'

'Nonsense. I watched your heroics today from the safety of my tower. That dragon has kept us prisoner here for the past ten days or so. Had you not slain it, it would not have been long before the creature turned its evil intentions on us. You risked your life for your people, King Bandred, of that you should be proud. Although, with the presence of the famed sorceress Amaleh di Varian, I was a little surprised that you put yourself at such personal risk.'

We both looked towards Amaleh who, even in the dim light, shone out – her pale features and glistening hair setting her apart from the crowd. Without taking my eyes from her, I responded, 'Her power must be preserved, Lord Rulan. If I do nothing else, I should protect her. The task that awaits her is a considerable one.'

'Oh, yes, yes, the valuable must always be protected. But all the same, King Bandred, to trap one that is so obviously capable and free …' he trailed off, in deep thought for a moment. 'You are aware, are you not, of the tale of *The Firebird*?'

Tearing my eyes away from Amaleh, I shook my head. Lord Rulan drew closer.

'It is a moral tale, Bandred, a tale that originates from the Eastern Kingdom and tells of a hero – a young man full of his world, who captures a magical glowing bird. Initially charmed by the bird, he later blames it for his troubles, and so the bird becomes both the blessing and doom of its captor.' He paused, waiting for my response.

'But this is real life, Lord Rulan,' I answered. 'She is not a bird and I, as much as I should like to believe your flattering words, am no hero.'

His face broke into a smile again and he slapped me on the back. 'You may well be right, Bandred, and anyway, at present there are more important things to attend to – so, here, let me fill your cup.'

Whether it was the generous measures of drink Lord Rulan poured, one after the other, or the atmosphere of the castle itself, I felt the troubles of the past weeks slip away. As the evening wore on and the dancing began, I noticed Amaleh looking, more than a few times, in my direction. Seizing the opportunity, I walked across the hall and held out my hand. Saying nothing, she rose and, placing her hand in mine, slowly we began to dance. Turning first one way, then the other, the music drawing us together as we moved. Gradually it sped up and then we were twirling round, I holding her waist, she my shoulders, no longer separate but a single unit, our hearts beating, our faces flush. It was as if a dream had descended on the castle that night – an enchanting dream that lasted until first light.

Our day's rest had been all too brief, but I was determined that we should delay no further. Lord Rulan kindly offered the service of some of his men to take the place of those lost to us and also to allow those who had been affected by disease to recuperate. The weather, not being too severe, would allow us to use the Andaaja Pass, a safe means of passage through the heart of the Fincormach Mountains and a short cut into the Northern Kingdom, which would save us valuable time. Just as we were leaving, however, a messenger arrived with a letter from the palace at Villiandra. Immediately I recognised it as my brother, Alvah's, hand. This is what it said:

My dear brother,

    I hope with all my heart that this letter finds you in good health and that you have the spirit to overcome the ever-increasing evil with which the Four Kingdoms is faced. Forgive me for burdening you further, but there are things of which I think you should know.

    Since your departure, the palace has become increasingly dark. Lord Dedren seems preoccupied and withdrawn, only appearing from his chambers to saddle his horse and leave the castle for daylong rides that bring him home weary and ready for bed. When I talk to him, he waves me away with his hand and stares into the distance from red-rimmed eyes. I fear that he is losing his mind and that perhaps this dark force with which we are confronted is sending him mad with worry. As a result, with no clear command, the soldiers have become lazy, spending their days drinking and lounging around. This is of particular concern as, recently, our scouts have returned with news of a vast fortress on Arken Island inhabited by all manner of strange creatures, including dragons. I had understood such a fortress situated in this very spot was destroyed after Ganzicus' death, so can only imagine it is the work of magic that has restored it with such speed. The scouts have also reported a number of dragon attacks throughout the Kingdoms, with whole villages being burned to the ground.

    Closer to home and of no less concern I have knowledge that the palace staff, those who you sent into the villages, are planning a rebellion of their own. I have a real fear that unless we can rally the garrison, we may well lose our foothold on the palace. And so, Bandred, I beg you to let me take the lead. I know I am young but I have the respect of the men and know I can succeed in a defence if needs be.

I await your reply with anticipation.

Your most respectful servant,

Alvah

I passed the letter to Lord Rulan and when he had finished reading said, 'I am concerned about Lord Dedren. He was most upset at my insistence that he stay on as steward of the palace. Perhaps this, together with the pressure of the threat, has thrown him into a depression. I do hope he will recover soon.'

A puzzled look appeared on Lord Rulan's face.

'The last time I saw your father, shortly before his death, I went to visit him in his chambers. When I reached his door, I heard raised voices from inside. Not wishing to intrude at so delicate a moment, I hesitated a while, wondering what to do. Suddenly, the door flew open and Lord Dedren strode past, his face as dark as thunder. He seemed not to notice me. I entered the room and saw your father looking deeply

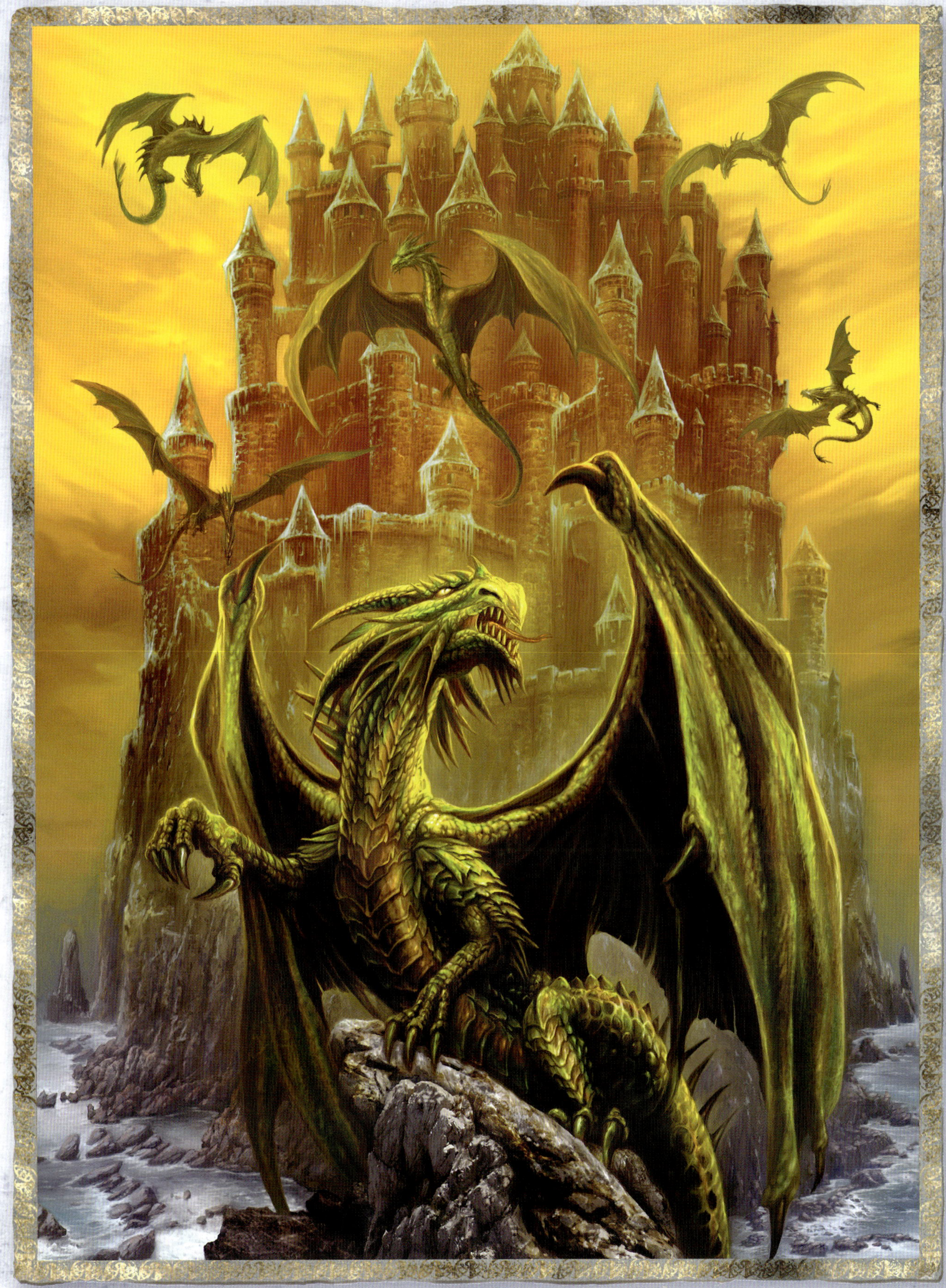

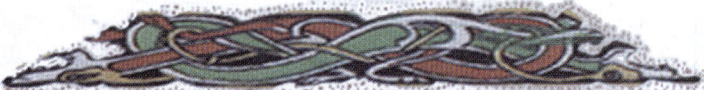

Arken Island

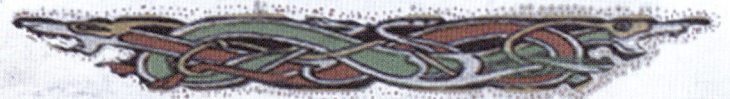

troubled. I enquired whether anything was the matter and he gave an enigmatic reply: "a little power can be a dangerous thing" were his words. At the time I thought he was talking about the fact that Lord Dedren was all too willing to show his anger, but, on reflection, perhaps he meant something more sinister.'

This I found difficult to believe. 'Lord Dedren is notoriously explosive. He and my father were always arguing. They were close. My father trusted him implicitly – why else would he have given Lord Dedren the role of my guardian after his death?'

'I don't know,' replied Lord Rulan.

'I think it would be a grave mistake to push Lord Dedren into a deeper depression by further relinquishing his control. I will write him some encouraging words of our successes. And although I am saddened by the stance of the villagers, without real leadership, they pose little threat. I shall inform Alvah of my decision.'

The letter to Alvah was tricky. Not wanting to take his concerns lightly, I had to give them some credence, but I had known Lord Dedren all my life and relied on him a good many times. He would rally round, I was sure. I had seen his black moods before and they never lasted long.

Chapter Seven

A Warning

Finally we were ready to leave the castle and, after saying our farewells, made the short journey to the ancient portal that would lead us into the mountains. The doorway was surprisingly small but no less dramatic because of it. Intricately carved, it featured on its keystone the arms of Lord Rulan's ancestral family – a column entwined with two serpents. I knew these to be the symbols of fortitude and wisdom. They served him well, I mused. The morning was cold and bright, but, as we departed the outside world and moved carefully down a steep slope that led into a rocky tunnel, the light faded. Only the faintest glimmer shone from the dim hand-held torches of our guides and the men were quiet as they adjusted to their new and strange surroundings. Mile after mile we walked, deeper and deeper into the mountain until the noises of our trooping: the marching feet; the trotting horses; and the low rumble of weapons as they bounced along the uneven path, echoed louder and louder, and we became aware our route was widening.

Before leaving his castle, Lord Rulan had told us that deep in the heart of the mountain we would pass through a natural cave, and, although not giving much away, was most insistent that when we reached the spot, we stop to rest awhile. Although keen to make as much progress as possible, I had not the heart to refuse his request. So when our guides called a halt and began to light the large lamps, I knew we had reached that place.

As the first flames leapt into life a kaleidoscope of colour burst into view. What looked like centuries and centuries of the most exquisitely coloured mineral deposits hung from the cave's roof. This was indeed a spectacular sight, made more so by the fact that we had been unprepared for such a display. Everyone stared, clearly in awe of the beauty that surrounded them. Amaleh, in particular, was much taken by the place, and commented on how untouched and precious it seemed. Impulsively, she thrust her Orb upwards and chanted a spell. A thousand sparks flew forth each reflecting the multitude of colours on display. Everyone gasped — it was a moment of pure wonder and a rare treat for the eyes of those who had become used to trying to forget, not remember, what they had seen.

And so, when we reluctantly left the cave, the men were in good spirits and marched with speed along the natural pathway that led towards the end of the pass. I travelled alongside Amaleh, pleased to be in her company and pleasantly surprised that, for once, she seemed willing to accept mine. After a while, the path sloped upwards until, on reaching its peak, we were blinded by a sudden shaft of sunlight, indicating that our journey through the Andaaja Pass had come to an end.

On leaving the mountain's interior, we assembled on a rocky ledge overlooking a deep crevice and beyond that the northern mountain range. My first impression was how different this side of the mountain was from that which we had left. Everywhere I looked, sheer cliffs sheathed in ice presented their austere and impenetrable faces. Lord Rulan's guides were to travel with us no further, but before they left, they pointed out a downwards track. This led to The Bridge of Trethian, a narrow pass across which we could traverse the crevice and reach the northernmost range and, beyond that, the Labyrinth of Fire. So, bidding our guides farewell, we set off.

Despite the bitter cold we made good progress and, after a short while, reached the crossing point — a narrow bridge high above the depths of the fathomless void below. From this position the view was exhilarating. We were surrounded by mountains; their power and majesty emphasising the fragility of the bridge that stretched out in front of us. Amaleh demounted and offered to lead the troops across. I decided to accompany her, despite knowing that I would find this part of the journey particularly gruelling. I had no head for heights and this together with the narrowness of the bridge would make it difficult for me to endure. We set off slowly and after a short while a trail of troops followed behind, snaking into the distance as far as the eye could see.

This part of the journey was slow and we were making little progress. To make matters worse a mist had built up making it difficult to make out the path ahead. I noticed that from time to time the mist cleared, but always it returned. It didn't make sense and I threw Amaleh a worried glance. Without responding verbally she halted the troop and lifted her head, as if smelling the air.

'We're not alone, Bandred,' she warned.

'I'll ready the weapons,' I replied.

I raised the command by blowing the horn, and then moved back down the line. Although we had left some of the bulkier weapons with Lord Rulan, we still had the *The Kronson*, which could be used to bring a dragon down, and *The Mazool*, with its poison-tipped shaft, could be used to inflict a fatal wound. After a flurry of activity the machines were ready and all we could do was wait.

Intense cold penetrated our garments and probed our flesh. All concentration turned inwards to cope with the pain of our chilled limbs and I wondered how long we could bear it. Gradually the mist cleared again and with it came warmth. Despite what this indicated, I felt a flood of relief as sensation returned to my limbs. Still we waited for the enemy to reveal itself, but all was quiet and again the mist closed in. Perhaps Amaleh had been wrong. I moved to the head of the troop and shouted for them to continue onward. However, Amaleh looked perplexed. Her eyes had narrowed to pinpricks and all her attention was focused on the swirl of dissipating mist ahead. As the troop moved forward, I was aware of something overhead. Looking up I realised we were now beneath the vast belly of a creature that moved silently through the air. As soon as it passed, the mist closed in again, and I found it necessary to halt the troops once more.

The creature was all but invisible, its pale skin blending perfectly with the environment in which it reigned. Our weapons were powerless if we could not see our target. I dreaded to think how vulnerable we were in such an exposed position. Soon enough, cries from further down the line signalled its first attack.

'The mist disappears as it approaches,' Amaleh remarked, 'It is its breath that clears the way. If we stay in position it will not identify us until after we know it is coming. Our only chance is to sit and wait for its return.'

Amaleh was right, however, not wanting to fire the poisoned shaft without having a clear view of the beast, I ordered that *The Kronson* be readied, hoping that by disabling the creature with mesh nets, I would be able to achieve a successful attack. Silently as it approached and the mists cleared again, I gave the signal for the nets to be released. They flew towards the dragon, but, stiff and inflexible from the cold, fell short of their target. We watched as they dropped, past the bridge into the crevice below. But the movement had caught the dragon's attention and it let forth a huge ear-crushing roar. There was nowhere to run and as we fell to the ground, the enraged creature spat shaft after shaft of red-hot fire into our defenceless rank. And so, despite not yet having a clear view of the creature, I decided to use *The Mazool*. Aiming the poisoned shaft high, I released the arrow. But the dragon saw it coming and changed direction. Again we flung ourselves to the ground; again the creature let forth its scorching spits.

Realising we were fighting a losing battle, I signalled to the men to run for cover. It was chaos. The mist made the passage forward terrifyingly difficult. All the while the dragon hounded us, flying backwards and forwards along our length and blasting fire indiscriminately at the men. The screams and shouts were terrible and many lost their lives. Finally the mist cleared and I realised I had reached solid land. I ran

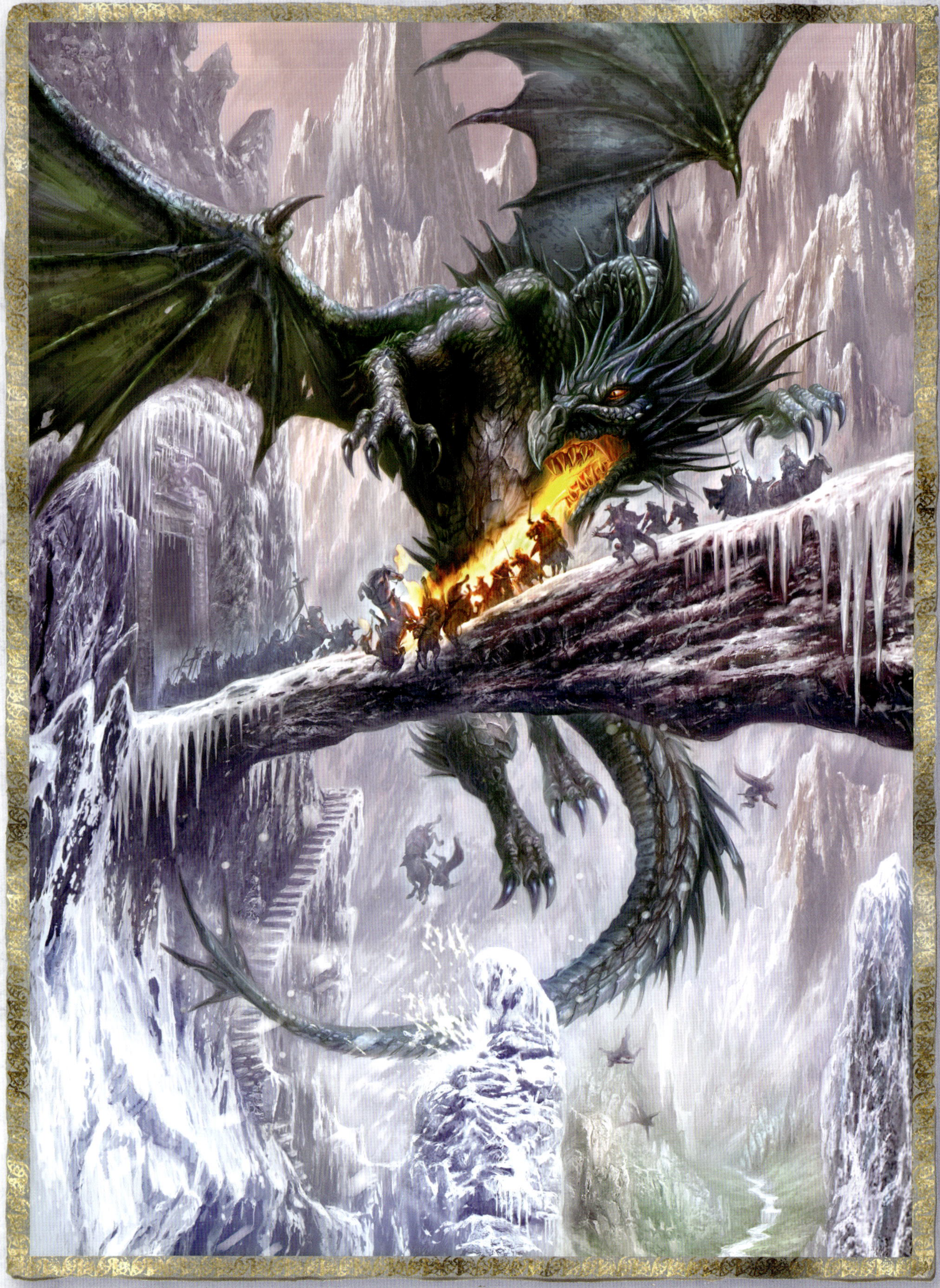

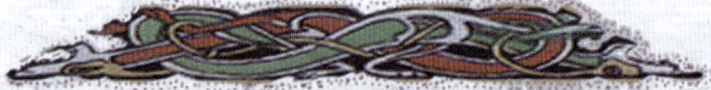

Attack on the Bridge!

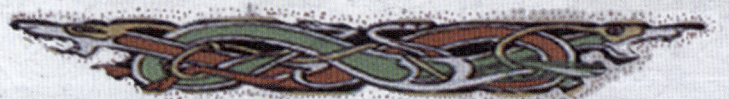

towards a large overhang under which we could take cover. One by one the remaining men staggered in, shattered by the extreme weather conditions and their terrifying ordeal.

I discussed our options with Captain Horzan. The dragon knew where we were, it would not let us leave. We decided to stay put until dark and then make a move, hoping that the dragon would grow tired of waiting. Amaleh disagreed and snatching up the Orb, left the cover of the cave. Standing fully exposed, she called to the dragon in a strange high-pitched voice I had not heard before. Soon it approached and for the first time we saw it in its entirety: it was a strange, ethereal creature, devoid of colour, skeletal in frame, but with huge eyes, as if it had spent many years in the dark. The dragon seemed enchanted by Amaleh's call and hovered in the air, in front of her. Amaleh went for the attack then. A single crack of the Orb gave out a bright light that struck between its eyes. There was no blood, no terrible screams and no fight for life. The creature merely slumped forwards into a huge lifeless heap.

A cheer went up in the cave and the men flooded out to claim their prize, but my eyes were on Amaleh. She was laying on her back, with her eyes wide open — a deathly pallor creeping across her skin. She was unconscious and barely breathing, so I ordered the men to carry her back to the cave. Everyone was quiet, wondering, no doubt, what had happened during the seemingly successful slaying to have caused Amaleh's collapse. I sat by her side, staring into her face, waiting for signs of movement. When they did not come, my heart was lost and I prayed for her revival. And so, although we were now within a short distance of the Labyrinth's entrance, we decided to light a fire and set up camp.

I stayed with her all night, not once allowing myself to entertain the thought that she may never awake. And just before daybreak my stubbornness was rewarded. She smiled upon seeing me.

'What does a woman have to do for a drink around here?' she joked, weakly. I lifted my water bottle to her lips. She sat up, apparently no worse for wear after her terrible ordeal.

'How long have I been asleep?' she asked.

'Long enough. Amaleh, are you well?'

'Of course,' she replied, 'That dragon was strong with magic, it was no natural creature, you know, and required much power to take its life, but I am fine now.' However, as she went to walk, she stumbled.

'Amaleh, you are still weak. I insist you sit down and rest.'

I was starting to feel impatient now. My initial concerns about her wellbeing satisfied, I was frustrated at her having jeopardised the quest. She was clearly exhausted, something I had impressed upon her to avoid from the outset.

'Me rest, Bandred,' she said sulkily, 'what about yourself? You look as if you haven't slept all night.'

Not trusting myself to speak, I strode off out of the cave to calm down.

Chapter Eight

The Labyrinth of Fire

So great had been the loss of life at the Bridge of Trethian, the final stretch of our journey was conducted in silent reflection. As we battled onwards through snow and ice, I watched Amaleh carefully. She seemed tired and withdrawn, but I was too angry with her to express my concern. If she were unable to successfully perform the materialisation spell on the Labyrinthine Dragon, we would risk not only our lives but also those of our people. She seemed aware of my mood and when she spoke, addressed her comments to Captain Horzan. I was happy not to have to respond.

Finally, having navigated our way over the mountain, we consulted the map once again. Septimus had indicated that the Labyrinth could be identified by its distinctive entrance. He had drawn a rough sketch, but this did nothing to prepare us for the overwhelming sight that awaited our arrival. Set beneath a huge overhang, gigantic stalactites and stalagmites dripping with melting ice protruded from ceiling and floor, making it look like some ferocious beast's jaw. I understood perfectly how Septimus' curiosity had been aroused when he stumbled upon this display. It was little wonder he had decided to explore further into its depths. This final stage of our journey required magical, not physical, power, so, taking just a short time to rest, I ordered the troops to wait in the outer chamber and guard the entrance, while Amaleh, Captain Horzan and myself made the unknown journey through the Labyrinth alone. We needed to act speedily and travelling would be much faster with just the three of us. We bid farewell in some anticipation of what lay ahead.

The tunnels were wide and well made and we were able to walk with some speed towards our destination. Having taken a closer look at Septimus' plan of the Labyrinth before we left, Amaleh informed us it followed an ancient design — that of the seven-coils where, traditionally, each coil represents one of the seven bodies that move across the stars. I had heard of such labyrinths and knew that the ancients who had hewn this age-old rock would have meant it to be a symbolic journey, one that would bring truth and enlightenment to those who followed it. As we passed through the first two coils, travelling deeper and deeper towards the heart of our quest, I wondered what it would bring to us.

The third coil was long and it was some time before our route jumped back to the outermost coil. From here we worked our way inwards, aware that the temperature was slowly rising. It was as if we were travelling towards the fire-filled belly of a colossal stone dragon. Realising that finally we must be circling the centre, we followed the path outwards before winding in again. Here the tunnel turned sharply to the right and we reached the final passage that led to the anti-chamber.

The air was hot and thick and we drew breaths in greedy gasps. I could see a low opening at the end of the passageway and an orange glow reaching out to us. It flickered and threw our distorted shadows onto the rough stone walls. The heat was almost unbearable but, one by one, we crouched down and squeezed through. On the other side was a vast pool-filled cavern, full of glimmering light. At the far end a wall of flames, escaping from the chamber beyond, cascaded downwards like a waterfall, spraying sparks which sizzled and crackled as they hit the water's edge. A stone bridge divided the pool and led through the flames towards what appeared to be an entrance to the chamber beyond. Realising this was our destination, it was difficult to see how we could enter. After watching for a while, we noticed that the flames died down at regular intervals and so, decided, after the next burst had extinguished itself, that we would grasp the opportunity and run through. So great were the flames they obscured our view, and it occurred to me, in the moment before we left, we might well be running towards our death. But we had come this far and it was no time to lose heart. So, not knowing what to expect, we took our chance and covering our mouths so as not to choke, hurled ourselves blindly forward into our fiery fate.

The first thing I felt was a blast of searing heat. Flames jumped up the walls of the vast vaulted chamber creating a ring of fire in which we were now enclosed. I scanned for life, desperately searching for the mighty creature and noticed the others looking, too. However, there was nothing to be seen but a searing wind picking up debris from the ground and swirling it high into the air. Amaleh must have sensed something though, and with her staff, started drawing in the dust. As she made the magical marks, glancing each with the tip of her magical Orb, they sprang to life, lifting from the earth and surrounding her with a thick shaft of swirling light – energy that would help her perform the spell.

Still we could not see the Labyrinthine Dragon, but as Amaleh began her chanting, the swirling dust started to take shape. A vast sinewy creature, appearing almost fluid through its constant shape-shifting, flew around the chamber, its strange form occasionally shimmering as it came together, before breaking up again into an unrecognisable blur. It was a delight to see – we had found our dragon and Amaleh's magic appeared to be working. Gradually more and more of the dragon took shape, but I could see Amaleh was becoming weary. Desperate not to lose control, she drew more symbols, working faster and faster, chanting louder and louder until suddenly, the creature became whole, crackling and glittering with the unmistakable vital energy of life's force.

So captivating was this vision we were, at first, barely aware of the dark ghoulish creatures that were filling up the chamber, surrounding the already disintegrating dragon with their hideous forms. Soon we were dodging their low swoops, running this way and that, all the time trying to avoid the flames that leapt out towards us and tried to catch us in their incandescent arms. Suddenly, Captain Horzan and I were seized from behind. Amaleh, in her trance, seemingly oblivious to what was happening, continued with her magic, but the dragon was disappearing again and then, from the midst of the flames, Count Veldspar stepped into view.

'This time you die, King Bandred,' he roared, 'but first, a demonstration of my infinite power.' From beneath his cloak he revealed the Amulet and directed it towards the Labyrinthine Dragon. Shards of light leapt from the Amulet, gathering in a single stream that penetrated the creature and pulled it together with such skill and magnificence that I could only wonder at the power contained within. The Labyrinthine Dragon shimmered gloriously in the firelight. Its eyes were bright and conveyed such compassion that, for a moment, I thought we were to be saved. But this vision was all too brief. Holding the Amulet to his lips and chanting, Count Veldspar worked his evil. In a flash the creature was again transformed. This time into the most grotesque figure imaginable. Sharp bones protruded leathery black skin. Jaws dripped with foul-smelling bile. Gone was the enlightening spirit and in its place evil spewed in one almighty roar. Amaleh, however, seemed not to have noticed Count Veldspar's arrival and was surprisingly calm. Responding to the magical power surrounding her, she dropped the Orb, fell to her knees and stretched her arms out towards the now hideous creature. I shouted for her to make her escape, struggling against my captors as I did, but to no avail. Count Veldspar, clearly pleased with his work, turned to me laughing.

'You are lost, King Bandred,' he said scornfully. 'Everything is mine.

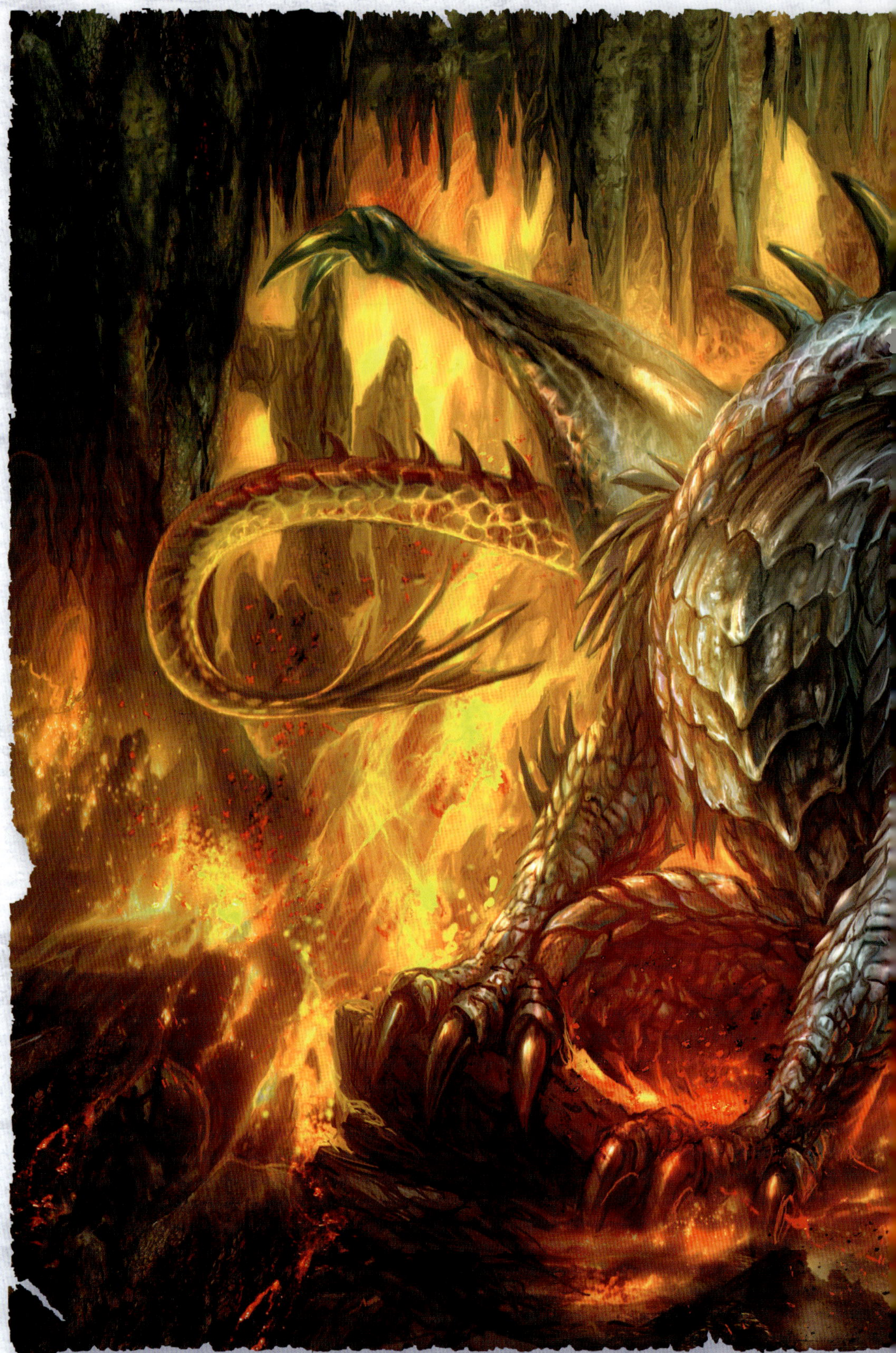

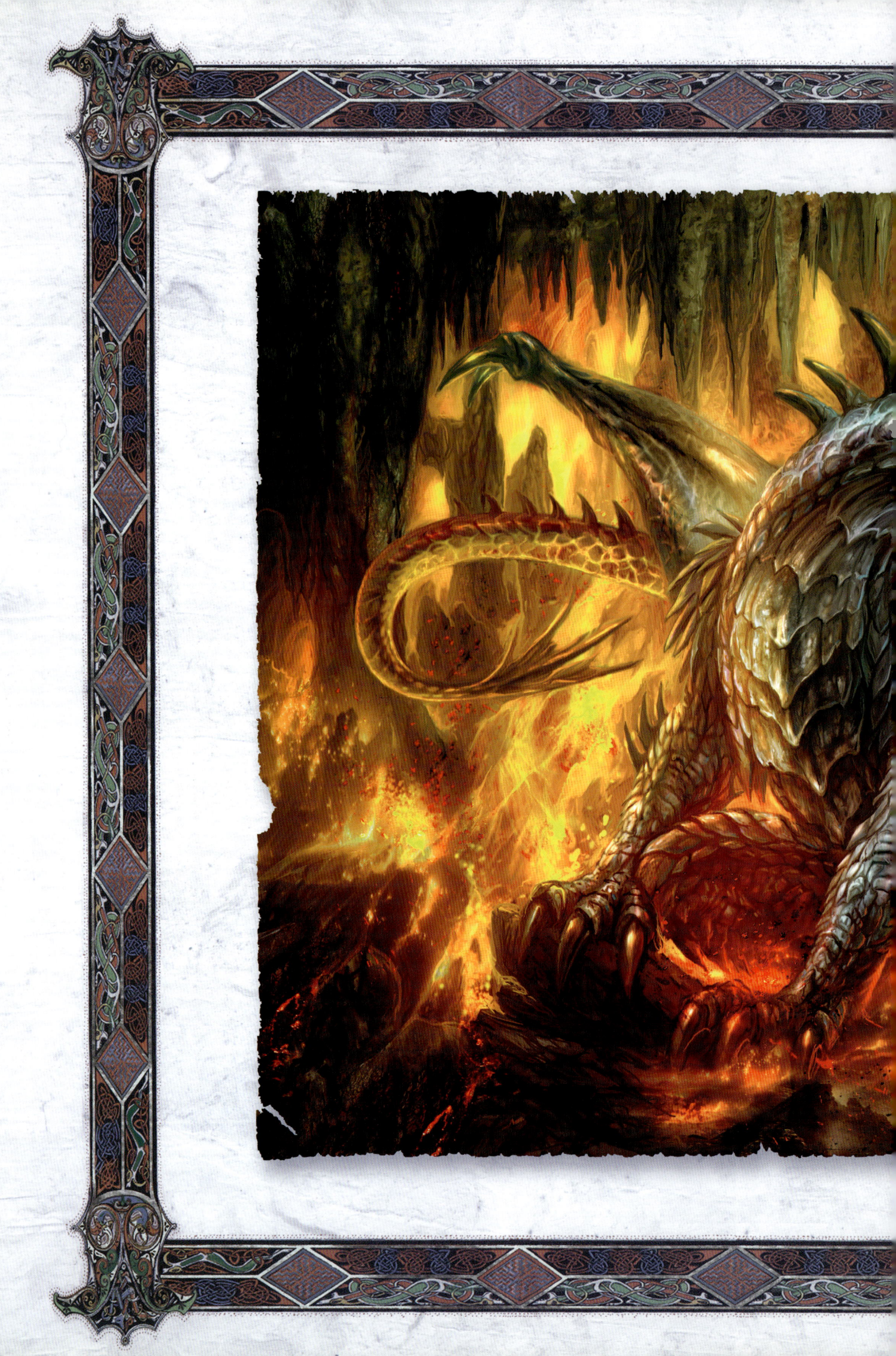

Dragon of the Labyrinth

From my fortress at Arken Island I will prepare the final attack against your palace at Villiandra. And the Sorceress? I shall need a mate. One with such powers as hers will suit me fine.' He turned to Amaleh, and offering her the Amulet said, 'Come here, golden one. Show your new master what you have learned.'

I watched her closely. At first she reeled from its power, almost falling into a swoon again. Then, regaining her balance, she held it to her lips in the very same way Count Veldspar had moments earlier, and muttering her spell, directed it towards Captain Horzan.

'No,' I screamed.

But it was too late. A shaft spat forth and hit the Captain in the chest. His body reeled with the impact and his captors let him go. I watched, fear rising in my chest, as he slumped, dead on the ground. I looked back to Amaleh. Again she held the Amulet to her lips and when she turned towards me, I knew I must escape. Using all the strength I could muster, I heaved myself backwards, pulling my captors with me into the wall of scorching flames behind. Again the shaft flew forwards from the Amulet, but, missing its target, pierced the wall instead, causing shards of heated rock to shower down upon us. With this my captors released their grip and I took my chance. Rushing through the fire-filled entrance and back into the anti-chamber, I made my escape. Round and round I ran, hearing the shouts of my pursuers getting quieter and quieter, all the time my heart heaving with the terrible failure of our quest.

But it was to get worse. When finally I reached the entrance chamber, instead of the much-needed backup, I found carnage. Piles of massacred bodies lay on the chamber floor. It was a pitiful sight and my heart ached with pain. But I had no time to grieve. I had to find somewhere to hide.

In no particular direction I hurried away from the Labyrinth, my only desire being to escape the intense evil I had encountered there.

I knew not how the evil had possessed Amaleh; I did know that she would have killed me if I'd stayed. After a while I found cover in a rocky crevice and rested awhile to gather my thoughts. Captain Horzan's death was devastating. He had been a stable figure throughout our journey, offering constant support. I felt his loss greatly. And now, with the Amulet, the Labyrinthine Dragon and Amaleh in Count Veldspar's power, our quest had surely failed. As I sat, I felt intensely cold. I knew if I was to survive I must keep moving, although, with no food or shelter I would not last long. So staggering this way and that, full of despair and despondency, I wandered, throwing myself to the careless whims of the chilling air.

I know not for how long I walked or what it was that caused my final collapse, only that I awoke feeling warm and relatively comfortable in the company of the remaining troops. They were hiding in the outbuildings of an ancient ruined castle they had stumbled across as they made their escape. Apparently, knowing that we too would encounter trouble at the hands of Count Veldspar, they had kept up a constant search for the three of us, eventually finding me half buried in snow. I told them of the events in the Labyrinth and of their Captain's death. All stood silent at this news, clearly shattered by the sad turn of events. I told them that their loyalty and courage was admirable and that they had carried out their duties to the highest standard and with unswerving dedication, but beyond that I knew not what to say. It was my job to lead, but where to and how? I had no answers. I could not contemplate returning to Villiandra a failure and, anyway, it would be impossible to fight against the force that was to be encountered on Count Veldspar's return. There had to be some other way — this could not be the end of my great family's reign.

Later that night, when I had forgotten the cold and drifted off into sleep, it was Septimus' face I saw. Amaleh was standing behind him and he was beckoning for me to join them, but as I walked, Amaleh turned into a bird. Not the brightly coloured bird of Lord Rulan's tale, but a raven, that, despite screeching into Septimus' ear, he seemed not to hear. And so, when I awoke, I knew what I must do. I decided to take a journey into the unknown — to that place beyond Gorenson Crag, the Palace of the Elders, visited only by fading magis and to which Septimus had retired. As far as I knew, no ordinary person had ever travelled there, but where else could I turn? I resolved to send half the remaining troops back to Villiandra to report to Lord Dedren the news of Count Veldspar's proposed attack, and take the rest with me to the Palace of the Elders and wherever else that might lead.

Chapter Nine

The Search for Truth

We awoke to a clear morning, said our farewells and set out on a path that led into the little-known lands of the northernmost regions. Here the landscape was unfamiliar. Virtually featureless apart from the vast natural ice sculptures that dripped and glistened in the sun, I had never seen such a strange and beautiful place. Far in the distance was the towering peak of Gorenson Crag and it was towards this we travelled.

During the journey I had time to collect my thoughts. There were certain things about which I was confused. How did Count Veldspar know of the Labyrinthine Dragon? And Amaleh — there had always been something not quite right about her behaviour towards me — she had seemed nothing short of contemptuous of me at times. Why was that? The further we walked, the more and more I thought, and I just kept coming back to three things: only Amaleh knew of the Labyrinthine Dragon; only Amaleh had access to the map; and, excepting members of the High Council, only Amaleh had known where the Amulet was. What if her thirst for power matched that of the young Count Veldspar and in him she had met her true match? My mind raced with these maddening thoughts. What a formidable pair they would make. By the time the shout went up from the scout that we were in sight of the Palace, I was consumed with passion, devoid of any rational thought.

Like an oasis in a desert, the Palace of the Elders shimmered into view. It is not known who built the Palace or indeed when it was constructed — as far as anyone knows it has always existed. It is a place between this world and the next — a magical place with a stillness and quietness that demands respect. Leaving the troops to set up camp, I made the final steps of the journey alone. As I approached, I felt calm. Set within its exquisitely carved façade were huge ice doors that seemed to melt away before my eyes and lead me into the vast entrance hall beyond. There, a small creature, almost childlike in appearance but with the mannerisms of an old man, appeared. Running ahead, he led me along a corridor full of statues of long departed magi towards another set of doors. There he told me to wait.

After a short while, the doors swung open, revealing a cavernous hall, its walls lined with huge statues of dragons carved from ice. The vast room was furnished with just a single throne from which light shone in all directions being reflected from the iced surfaces all around. I blinked, adjusting my eyes to the incredible brightness and as I focused I could just make out the faintest outline of a man sitting upon the throne – a man I recognised and loved.

'Septimus!' I cried in relief.

Whether or not it was because he heard my voice, I do not know, but the form grew stronger and gradually he emerged.

'King Bandred,' he gasped, catching his breath, 'is it really you? This is no place for a living soul. Why have you come?'

His less than enthusiastic welcome and obvious frailty unnerved me. How could I possibly ask him to help? Again his image receded, fading first into nothing then, once more, back into a less than solid form.

'Septimus, had I any other choice I would not have come, but I have failed my people and know not where to turn. Our Kingdoms are under the evil influence of Count Veldspar. The Labyrinthine Dragon is in his command and Amaleh …' I broke off, unable to continue.

On hearing her name, Septimus' presence grew stronger.

'Is Amaleh safe?' he asked.

'She is with Count Veldspar,' I replied, but did not expand, unwilling to reveal the true nature of my fears.

'How is this?' Septimus inquired.

I recounted the events in the Labyrinth, still concealing the growing doubts I held, but Septimus read my thoughts. Suddenly, slipping back into his throne, his power once more diminished, he said, 'She is possessed. You must release her,' and then looking me directly in the

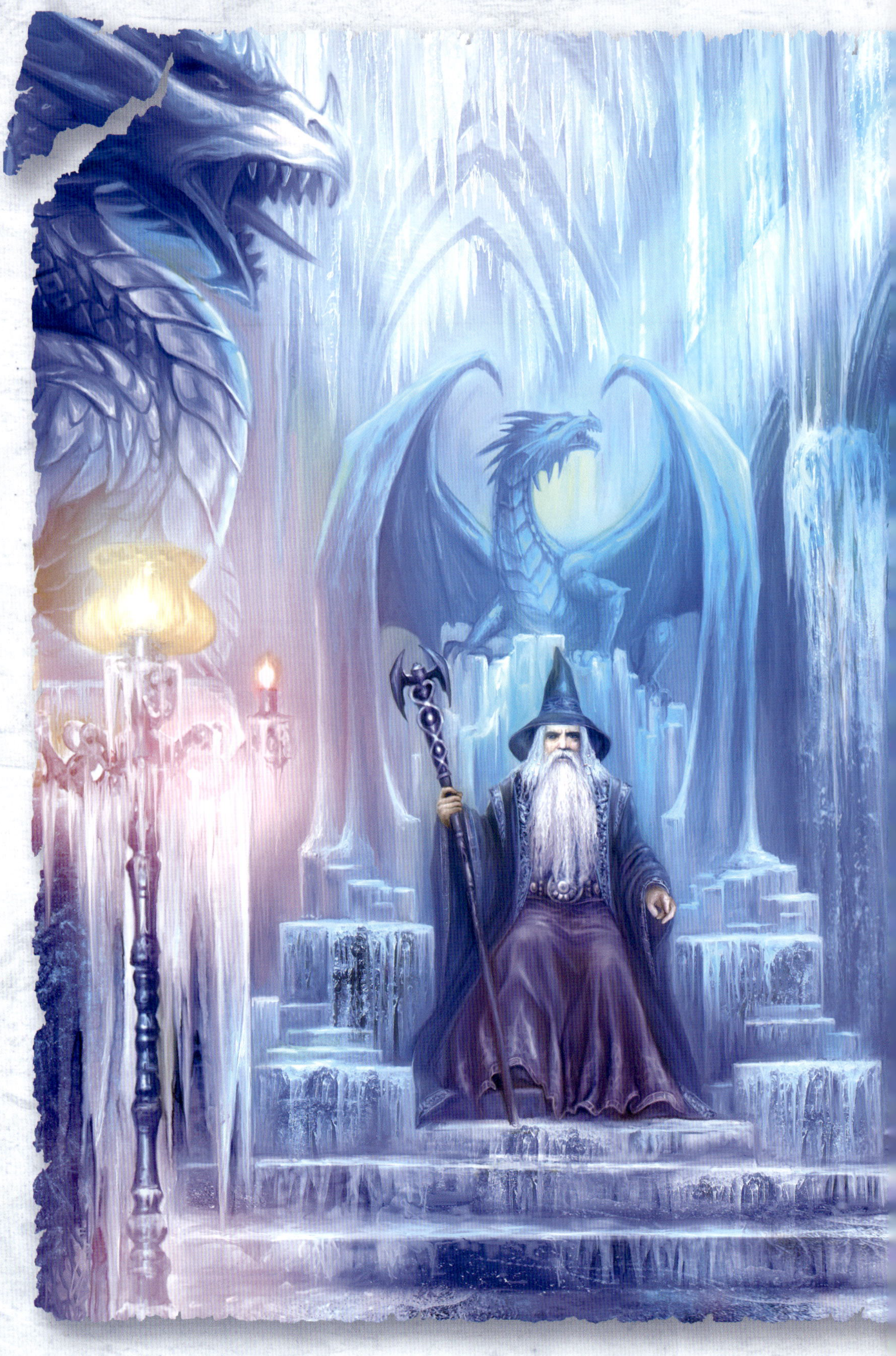

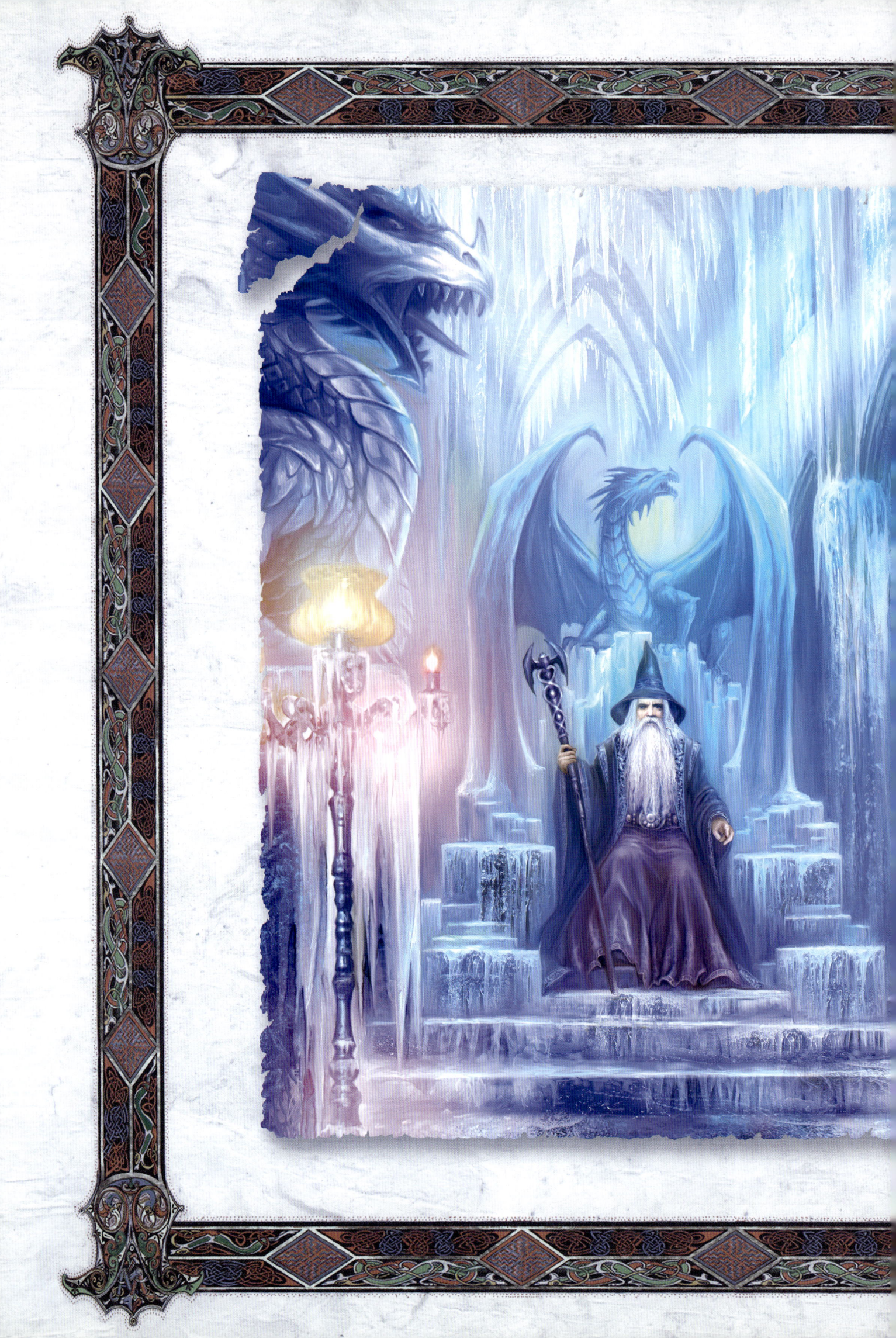

The Ice Palace

eye, continued, 'without your leadership and her talent, Bandred, you will fail.'

The throne was empty now, he had all but disappeared. I heard the door open behind me and knew it was time to leave. This was not what I had expected – it was not enough. Where was I to go from here? Reluctantly I retraced my steps back to the entrance hall where, once again, I was met by the creature. He ushered me towards the door, but before I left placed something in my hand.

'For the sorceress,' he said. 'For redemption, if she be true. Or death, if she be not.' Closing my hand around the object, I slipped it into a pocket and quickly stepped outside.

It was dark but torches guided me back to our camp. All was quiet save the night watchmen whose low voices provided comfort to what would prove to be a difficult night. Taking the object I had been given at the Palace out of my pocket, I held it up to the firelight to examine more closely. It was a tiny vial. Contained within were no more than a few drops of dark-looking liquid. Prising open the top, I smelled its contents. It was odourless. Septimus had indicated to me that he trusted Amaleh explicitly, but his servant's words had suggested this might not be the case. All night long I turned over the events of the past few weeks. So much had happened. What had I missed? I knew I must have been betrayed, but could think of no-one, save Amaleh, who would benefit from this new regime. She, alone, had the motive. And so, if this were true, I must kill her. However, I was not sure this was something I could do. Septimus had also talked of leadership. Feeling the sharp prick of humility, I stared into the fire.

Later, from out of nowhere, an old man appeared. I was sure I had not seen him before, but he insisted he was one of the watchmen and asked me, as I was up so late and chilling an hour, whether I should like a warm drink. I accepted and, on returning, he sat down with me by the fire.

'You're troubles are great are they not?' he inquired, seemingly ignorant of who I was.

Suddenly I wanted to talk. I spoke of Villiandra and the carefree life I had enjoyed there. I told of the support of Lord Dedren and of the deep friendship between my dear brother Alvah and myself. I moved on to how Count Veldspar's dragon attack had put an end to our golden times and about the guilt I felt that I had allowed the Amulet to be stolen. I told of Septimus' parting gift and the subsequent quest, of Amaleh and our plans for the Labyrinthine Dragon and, then, of the evil unleashed instead. I ended by telling him I had run out of options and of hope, and how now here I was trying to talk myself out of despair. And he listened, this ragged old man, with patience and without interruption, and when I had finished speaking he asked me a question.

'What is it you most desire?'

I thought this most strange, but finding relief in the fact that I had someone with whom to share my troubles, I answered, 'To deliver the Four Kingdoms of Vaarn from evil and for the Amulet to be returned.' But even as I spoke I knew this was not the truth. It was Amaleh di Varian I most wanted. From the moment I had set eyes on her in the cemetery, she had blinded me with her beauty and bewitched me with her power. But these were not the thoughts of a noble king. Septimus was right, Amaleh and I were honoured people. With my birthright and her natural gift, we both had an obligation to serve the realm. What right had we to our own private thoughts and dreams? I turned to repeat myself and to answer as a king, but the man was already hobbling off, shrouded in darkness in this strange and chilling land.

Chapter Ten

Dark Magic

Three days later, weary after a long trek back into the Eastern Kingdom, we marched towards the coastal city of Dansk, domain of the much-revered Lord Sulian. The journey had taken us along the icy valley paths of the Fincormach Mountains towards Lake Ornio and beyond, where we had picked up the path that followed the River Xhion to its estuary at the Pharamond Sea. During our absence, the weather had changed quite considerably and raintime was now upon us, drenching our garments and filling the skies with its ominous heavy clouds. I had visited Dansk on a number of occasions during my princedom. Its sheltered position in Blandyke's Bay ensured its status as the main commercial port serving both Eastern and Northern Kingdoms. As such, its streets were always bustling with traders and profiteers from far afield. Here, wealth and poverty lived side by side, making it an interesting and vibrant place to be. Now, as we walked through the gates towards the heart of the city, I saw it was much changed. Huddled figures lined the streets slumped in abject hunger and many of the dwellings were boarded up, as if shutting out, or in, I knew not which, some terrible secret. I had sent word ahead of our proposed arrival and we did not have to travel far before we were met by delegates. As we were led up towards Dansk Castle, I could not help but compare this reception to that I had received the last time I visited. That was a welcome full of fanfare and celebration.

At the castle we were greeted by Lord Sulian himself. His sombre manner told me he had much on his mind. So, after providing dry clothes and some much-needed food, it came as no surprise when he told us that a terrible disease was sweeping through the city. Apparently, some weeks previously, Count Veldspar had visited Lord Sulian in an attempt to persuade him to join ranks and take arms against me. When Lord Sulian declined, Count Veldspar seemingly accepted his decision, however, a short while after leaving, the fatal pestilence descended, attacking young and old, rich and poor alike. At present, only the castle itself provided a haven from infection. The situation in the city was becoming more and more serious daily, with huge numbers of people dying and no traders daring to visit.

When Lord Sulian had finished, the troops told their tale. Here, for the first time, I heard what they had endured at the hand of Count Veldspar during the surprise avalanche at the entrance of the Labyrinth. Boulders and rocks had fallen and, terrified the entrance to the cave would soon be blocked, the men ran out to defend themselves. Outside they faced a vicious attack. Multitudes of dragons swooped overhead, raining down on them a deadly mixture of fire and poison that caused much of the loss of life. The men tried to raise the alarm, but it took all their strength and power to defend themselves. Finally, seeing the huge number of fatalities, they admitted defeat. There was no organised retreat – everybody simply fled for their lives.

After the retelling of the two sorry episodes there was little left to say and we retired for the night, each of us in low spirits remembering the dead and wondering if there was anywhere in the Kingdoms Count Veldspar's malevolence had not yet spread.

The following morning I told Lord Sulian that if we were to help him and his people we must leave the city and continue with our plan to rescue Amaleh. He, having already grasped the seriousness of the situation, introduced us to the captain of a ship in which we could safely travel to Arken Island. An old and experienced man of the sea, Captain Drolan's ability to remain calm in the face of adversity was celebrated across the land. His vessel *Freelander*, the fastest in the region, had withstood many a serious storm. It was also equipped with a full armoury and I had little doubt it would provide us with the quickest and safest means possible to reach our destination. So, having little to carry aboard save a trunk of preparations that had belonged to Amaleh, we left the port with the morning tide.

Once at sea I inspected the contents of Amaleh's trunk and noticed that among the many remedies was a jar labelled *Fumnox*. This, I knew, to be a potent poison and wondered why ever she would carry such a substance. The memory of the dreadful pustules suffered by our soldiers during the early stages of our journey to the Labyrinth flashed through my mind.

The first three days of our voyage were largely uneventful. The waters were normal for the time of year – slightly choppy with the occasional thunderstorm – nothing Captain Drolan couldn't navigate. On the fourth evening, just before I retired to my cabin for the night, we spotted Arken Island on the horizon. After a short discussion with Captain Drolan we decided that I should try and sleep to preserve my strength, and that he would wake me just before first light.

I know not for how long I slept, but was awoken in the dark by the ship's mate and asked to hurry to the foredeck. There I found Captain Drolan pointing at the water. At first I saw nothing unusual. It was dark and I could just about make out the continuous movement of the inky black surface, but as I stared into the water's depths, I noticed it was heaving, heaving with serpents, their dark coils squirming this way and that.

'What are they?' I asked the captain.

'Their like I have never seen,' he replied.

As we stared, the serpents' movements became more and more frenzied, the water foaming as they forced their way towards its surface.

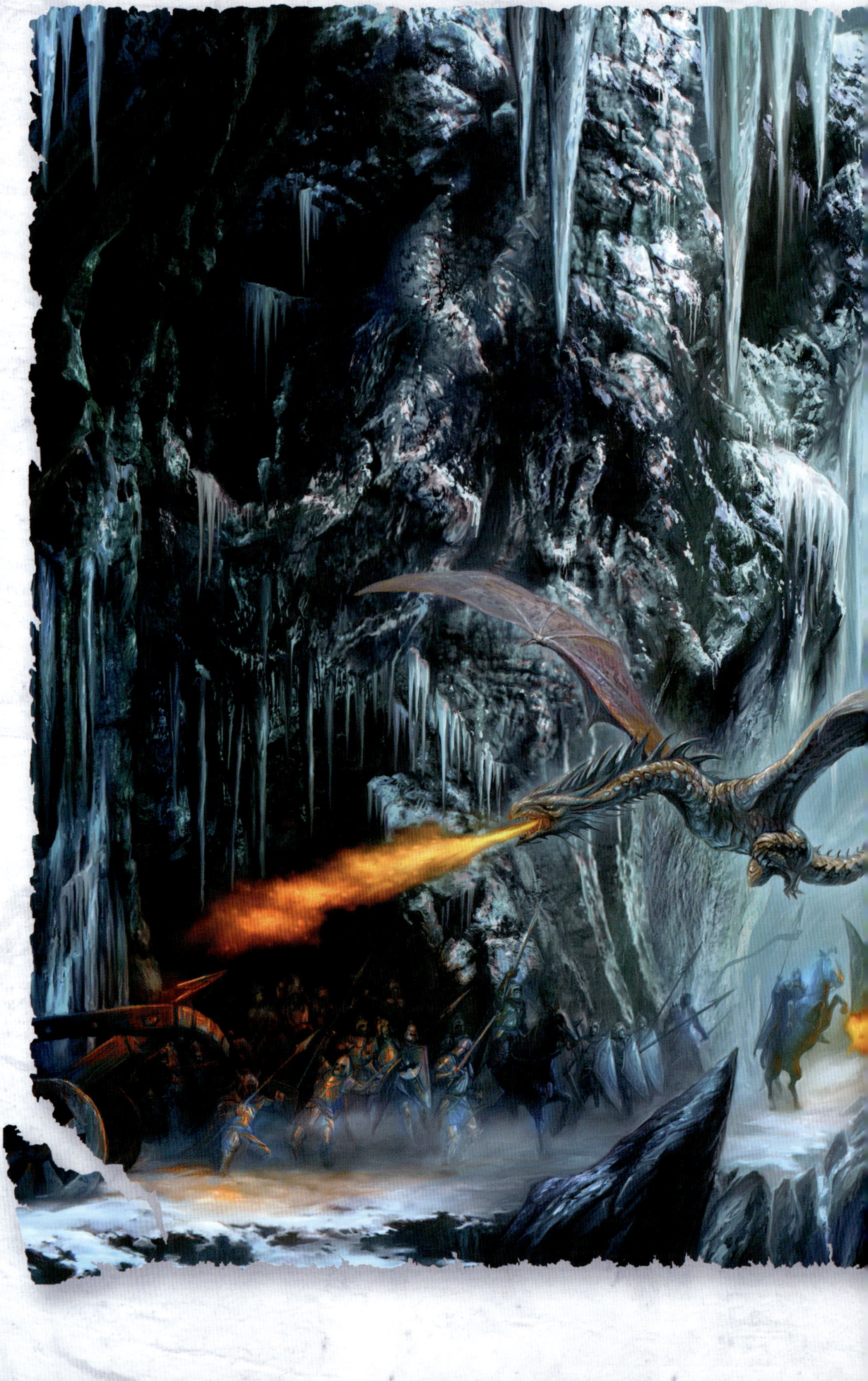

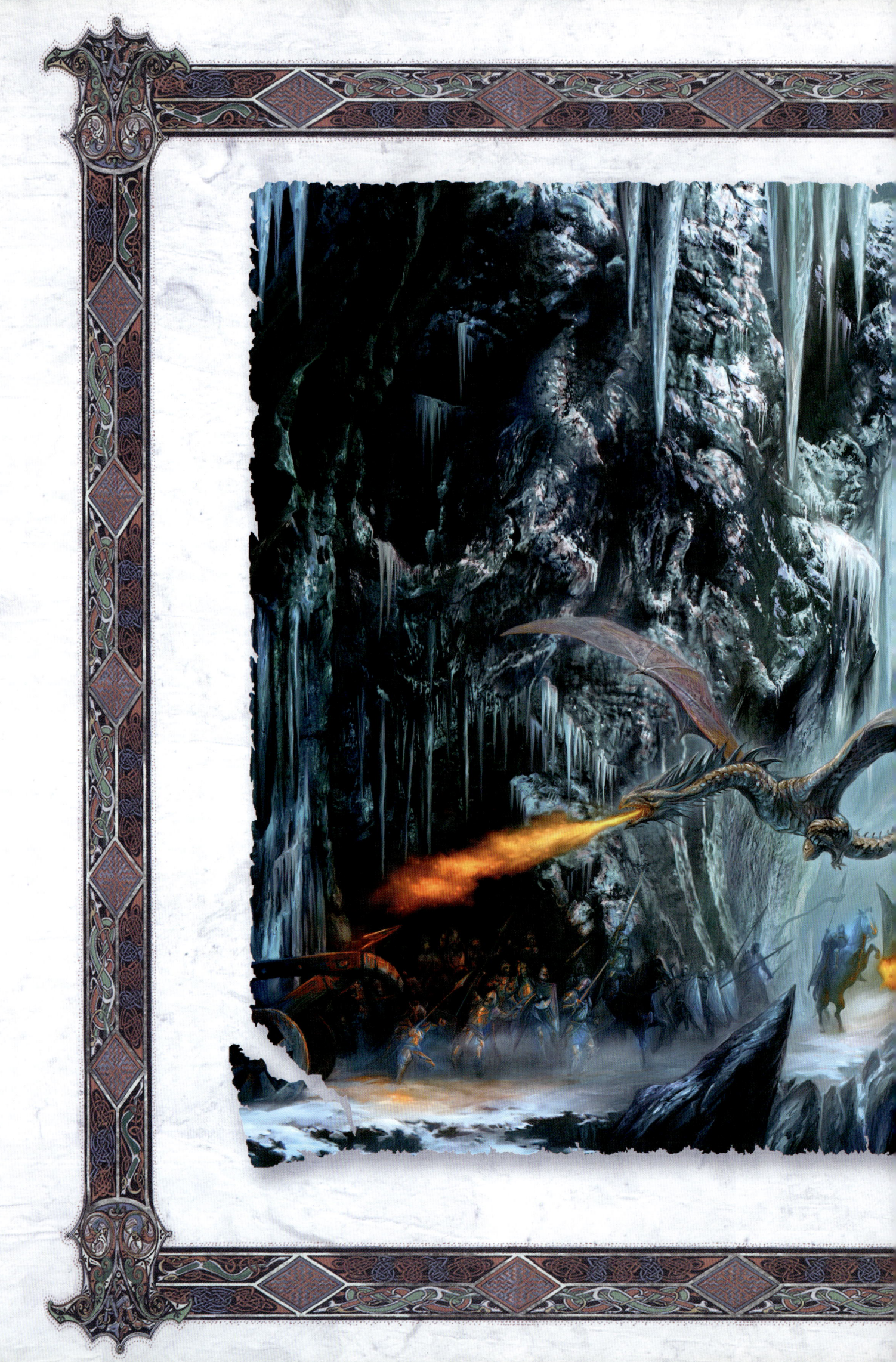

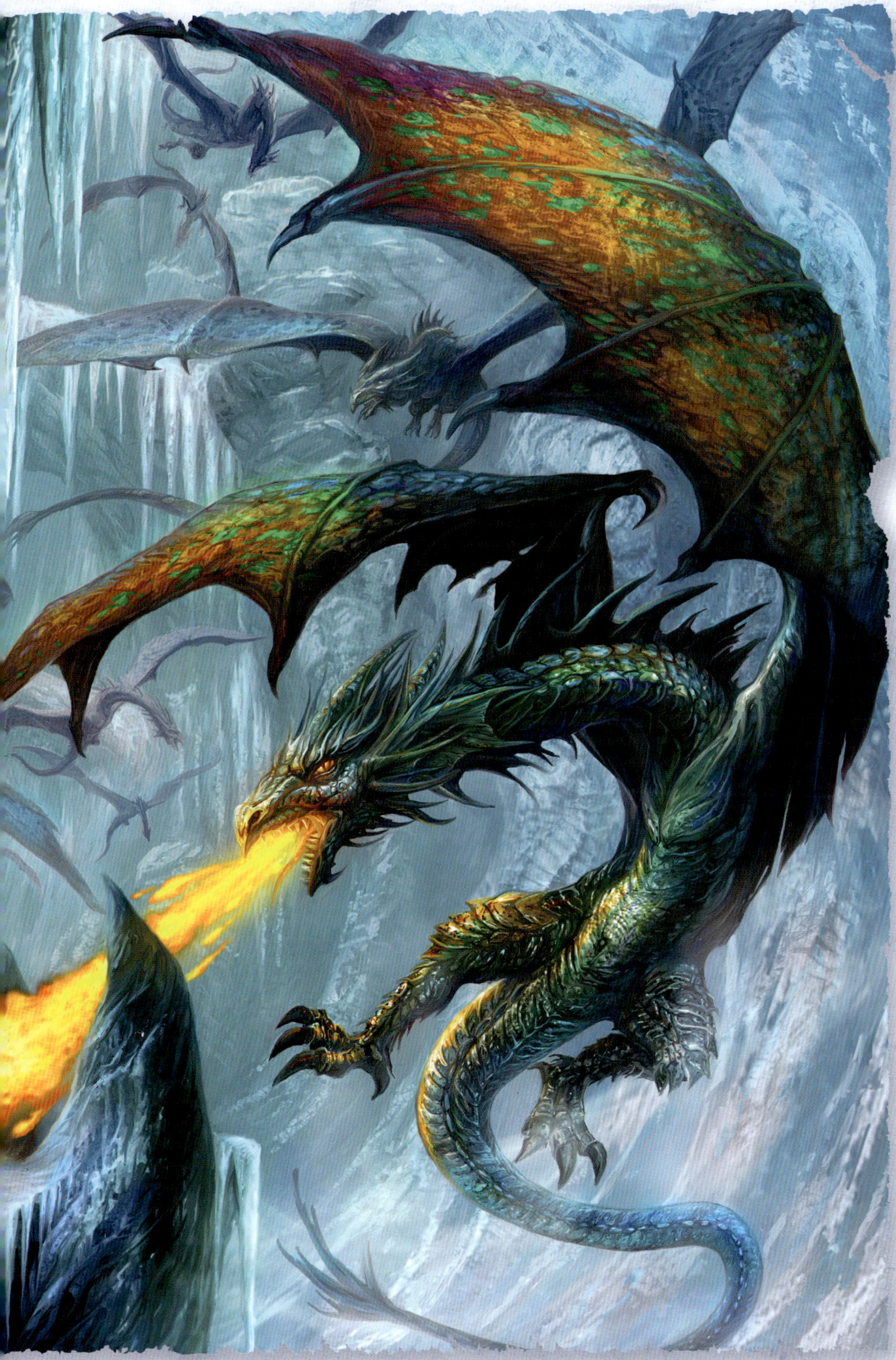

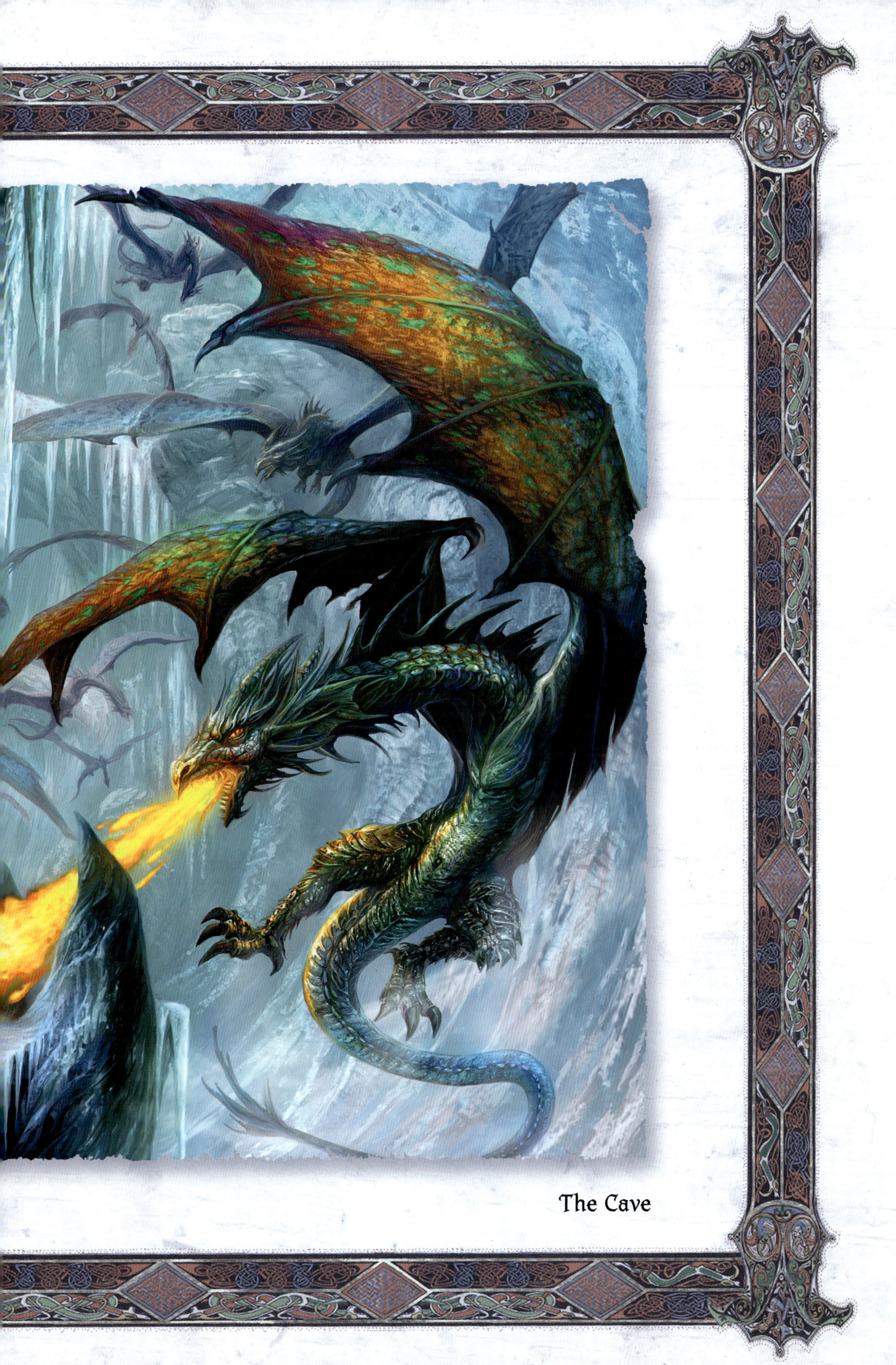

The Cave

Soon the ship was rocking violently from side to side. They seemed to be growing — and then I saw their jaws. Full of pointed fangs their snapping snouts shot out of the water, gasping for the air above the seething sea. I shouted for the men to arm themselves, but, even as I did, could see that arrows would have little impact on this mass of slithering bodies. Then I thought of Amaleh's poison. Without delay, I ran below deck, lurching this way and that as the ship was tossed about in the tumbling water. Everything not secured was hurtling along the floor, the trunk being no exception, and it was with great difficulty that I managed to hold it still long enough to find the jar.

Back on deck, I leaned far over the side of the ship to empty the contents overboard, but as I did, one of the serpents left the water, flapping a set of newly grown wings. I watched, frozen in horror as the creature took to the air, noting that its tail had receded into its now squat body and that its jaws were frighteningly voracious and fully-grown. As it snapped wildly about my arms, inflicting numerous bloody wounds, I noticed others were leaving the water too. Realising I must act quickly, I emptied the jar as best I could into the boiling mass and retreated to the foredeck to climb the mast and get a better view. As I gained height and therefore perspective I could see that the men, in a desperate attempt to control the onslaught, were shooting arrows at the airborne creatures. From the top of the mast I could see Arken Island, too.

We were not far off now and standing outside on a ledge jutting out from one of the towers, high above the craggy rocks below, I could just make out the shadowy figure of a woman, a woman I recognised. It was Amaleh, standing with her arms outstretched towards our ship and, no doubt, the flying serpents below.

Looking down, I noticed the poison seemed to be working. No more creatures were leaving the water and any movement there was seemed

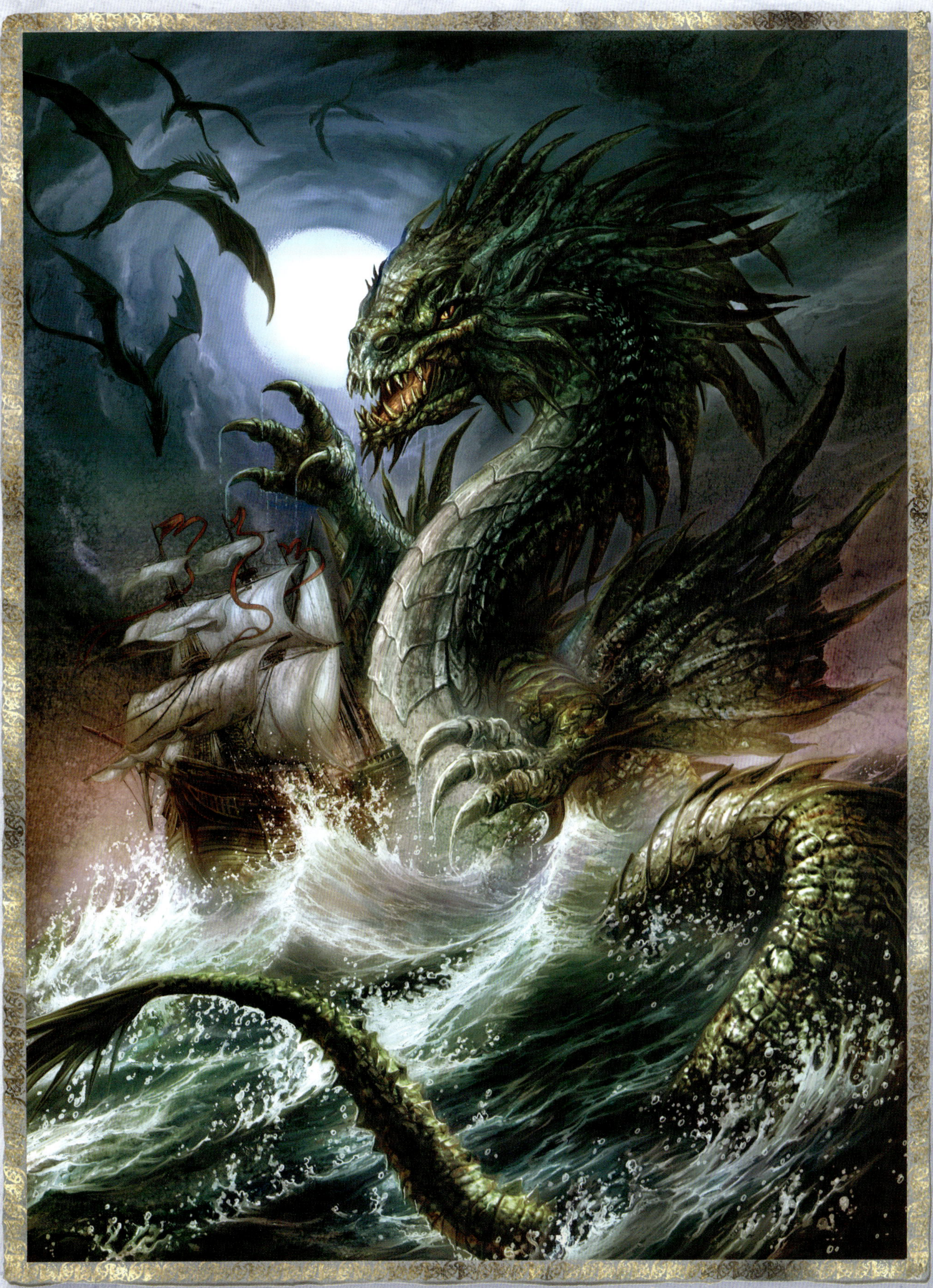

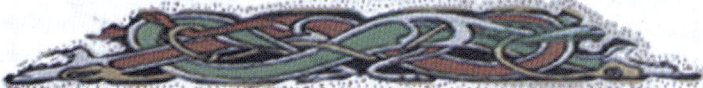

The Sea Serpent

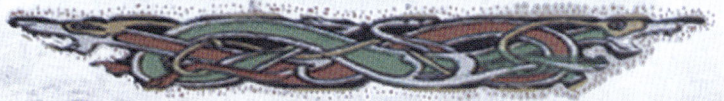

to come from those in the last throes of death. Back on deck, it was carnage. Many of the men were on the floor having been badly bitten, and once down, the creatures didn't cease their attack. Crawling to find cover, the men were leaving bloody trails that crisscrossed the deck and allowed the creatures to follow their scent. Pondering on how to overcome these creatures, I wondered, if they were the result of Amaleh's dark magic, what form they might next take?

Freelander's larger weapons were useless against these conjured spirits, so quick they flitted between the men, even the arrows missed their targets. I needed to break Amaleh's control over these vile creatures, but how? I could not reach her – the distance made that impossible. Then I had an idea. All of the creatures were now on the main deck. If we lowered the sails and positioned the ship so that they provided a barrier between Amaleh and her servant serpents, we might just break her hold. Hastily I issued the command, sliding down the main mast and rushing to the wheel myself. As the sails dropped into place, I spun the wheel and slowly the ship started to move. But not fast enough. Still the cries came from the deck, and I could see those men who were left standing were surrounded by the pernicious creatures, barely able to draw their bows. Finally, as the ship turned, the spell broke. Creatures fell amongst the exhausted men onto the deck. We watched transfixed as their hideous remains shrivelled back into those writhing, slithering, creatures of dark evil, and I ordered the men to throw them back into the water. Looking towards Arken Island, the figure at the tower turned and, without so much as a second glance, stepped back inside.

Chapter Eleven

Mortal Danger

The fortress on Arken Island presented a formidable sight. Three narrow towers dominated the rocky landform, reaching upwards into a thick mass of grey cloud that gathered forebodingly over the dragons' retreat. Having decided not to risk taking the ship too close for fear of being spotted, Captain Drolan had set anchor some distance off and I was carefully lowered in one of the dinghies into the water below. I noticed, in the cold grey light appearing over the horizon, the figures of three dragons flying in a circuit around the fortress. From time to time one of them disappeared into the clouds only to reappear moments later with the same steady flapping motion, scanning the area below. Fortunately for me, a dragon's eyesight is not at its best in half-light. I shuddered to think what might have befallen me if these creatures were alerted to my presence. As I rowed, a foul-smelling odour caught in my throat, forcing me to choke. Stopping to pull my cloak up around my nose, I breathed deeply into the musty fabric and checked that the vial given to me at the Palace of the Elders was still safe in my pouch. Fearing the power of Amaleh's possession I knew that to administer it I would have to catch her unaware. I did not allow myself to dwell on the possibility that Amaleh was not possessed and was merely acting according to her deepest wishes. At this time these thoughts could have no useful place in my mind. With determination I rowed through that dark sea with the rain falling in thick drops all around me, knowing that whatever happened next would determine the future of the Kingdoms.

Before setting off I had spotted an inlet to the north of the Island, just below the turret at which I had seen Amaleh, and it was here that

I moored my boat. Scrambling across the rocks towards an overhang in the rough stone wall, I hoped my movements would not attract attention from the dragons above. Exhausted from the physical exertion of rowing, I took a few minutes to catch my breath. By now the dull morning light was creeping across the vast expanse of water surrounding the island. Soon it would be light.

With no obvious entrance at ground level, I decided to scale the wall and enter through the first opening I reached. So, grasping at the stonework to find a firm foothold, I commenced the ascent. I climbed carefully and soon was almost within reach of a small ledge that jutted out from underneath the first opening. Making the extra stretch, I managed to grip its rough surface. However, the stone was wet and, in trying to position my right foot, I slipped. Loose rubble tumbled from the building onto the rocks below and I was left hanging, using all the strength in my arms to hold on. Suddenly I was aware of a shadow gliding slowly past. Out of the corner of my eye I could just make out the scaled underbelly of a dragon. Daring not to risk a move that would send more stone crashing onto the rocks below, I tried to remain as still as possible. This took a huge amount of physical effort, but eventually the dragon passed – it had not spotted me and for this I felt relief. Again I fumbled for a foothold and, this time, finding my place, was able to heave myself up through the opening into the darkness and the unknown.

As soon as I was inside I noticed the odour again. The stench was unbearable and I remember thinking that if ever evil had a smell, this was surely it. Quickly summing up my whereabouts I realised I was in a stairwell although it was like no other I had ever seen. Faint shadows danced in front of my eyes and I knew not whether they were real or imagined. Although terrified by the thought of having to travel further into this abyss, I nonetheless knew I must carry on. The ledge on which

I had seen Amaleh was much higher and to the right, three floors up, so I began, once more, to climb. As I ascended, the stairwell grew darker and, without a candle to light my way, I was forced to slow my pace, touching the walls to feel my way, round and round, higher and higher, only occasionally passing another opening into the main building and presumably another floor. As I approached the final flight, I stopped and, taking the small vial from my pouch, loosened the stopper. Suddenly, in an impulsive move, I pressed the object to my lips. My heart raced – I was not sure if I was capable of this. If Amaleh were to die … the thought was inconceivable so I blocked it from my mind, replaced the stopper and forced myself onwards. Finally, seeing the light from the next opening, I realised I had reached my destination. I turned right and stole silently along the corridor. Ahead was the entrance to a chamber. I knew instinctively that this is where she would be.

Opposite the entrance was an opening into what I assumed was the central courtyard of the fortress, it was through this the morning light now streamed. I knew I must hurry, but as I passed, I could not resist glancing through. It was an act I have regretted my whole life for words could hardly describe the depths of evil to which I was witness. I saw bodies roasting in dragon fire and phantoms tearing men limb from limb. I saw women and children … but I cannot continue. The monsters I have forgotten. The faces of the unfortunate people I have not. And so I turned from that scene with a newfound purpose and walked into the darkened room.

The contrast could not have been greater. First the smell of dusky roses flooded my senses, unlocking my memories and reminding me of our meeting, all those weeks ago, in the palace cemetery, when, full of life and spirit, she had chided me into action. Here, she lay asleep, dressed still in her white sorceresses robes. She was a picture of peace and innocence and I remember thinking that no-one who looked this pure could be evil. At that moment, I believed Septimus to be right. And to see her there, so quiet, so vulnerable – it was with great restraint I stopped myself from burying my head in her shoulder and weeping at what she had become. So quickly, before I had a change of heart, I took the stopper from the vial and poured the thick liquid into her mouth. Slowly her tongue appeared and licking her glistening lips, she took the potent magic in.

The relief I felt when Amaleh awoke was incredible. She told me afterwards that she lay there for some time, fully conscious but completely unaware of her predicament. She said it were as if she were floating away from the depths of darkest despair. She felt soft arms caress her body and the sound of gentle music fill her ears and, although she could see me and knew who I was, felt for a time as if she were suspended in a different world and could not be reached. But of this I was unaware. So anxious was I to see her conscious and restored, I did not allow myself to believe she might still be elsewhere. All I knew was that Amaleh was saved. She was back by my side and my thoughts turned to the task at hand. If we were to stand any chance of defeating the evil, we needed the Amulet. There was no time to lose. Helping Amaleh down from her bed, I asked her if she knew where it was.

'It is kept heavily guarded in Count Veldspar's chambers,' she replied.

'Do you think you can get it?' I asked.

'That shouldn't be difficult if Count Veldspar is absent. His servants trust me. I will go immediately. Wait for me here. I will return as quickly as possible.'

But as she turned to leave her exit was blocked.

'So, my lady, you have chosen the path of death,' Count Veldspar snarled. 'What a pity it is that you will not be present to share in my success. Rarely have I seen so much potential in one so young. And as for you,' he spat in my direction, 'what foolish whim brought you here? Oh, but I forgot, you're not powerful enough on your own are you? No wonder Lord Dedren enlisted my help.'

He must have seen the expression of surprise on my face and his dark face lit up.

'No,' he laughed. 'I don't believe it. You didn't suspect your uncle? At least I offered him the chance of leadership. All those years playing second fiddle to your "oh so fair" father only to become the faceless brains behind a juvenile puppet like you. What did you expect, King Bandred, gratitude?'

I felt dizzy with the sudden comprehension of it all. Of course, Lord Dedren had stolen the map, he had known where the Amulet was – I never once suspected him. I looked at Count Veldspar but could think of nothing to say. Lord Dedren – I had trusted him.

'But all that is a mere irrelevance,' Count Veldspar continued, 'I should be thanking you, instead, for giving me such a perfect opportunity to end your family's reign. Today we fly to Villiandra for the final battle. Lord Dedren has rallied troops outside the palace walls and with you out of the way, we will only have your brother and his inexperienced garrison to contend with. The Labyrinthine Dragon has already proved to be a valuable asset – as its commander I will prove to be the most powerful king this realm has ever known.'

'Over my dead body,' I said, suddenly finding my voice.

'That,' retorted Count Veldspar, 'will be my pleasure. There is only one death fit for a boy-king like you.' And turning to his guards he said, 'Throw him in the dungeon and take his lady with him. We can spare the Dragon of Remilia – I can just imagine what deadly sport it will make of them.'

The look on Amaleh's face was enough to tell me we were in mortal danger. I went to pull my sword from its sheath, but was immediately overcome by the guards. Amaleh, who had been captured also, was powerless. The guards pushed us roughly forwards, towards the dungeon and to our certain deaths.

Chapter Twelve

Kingship and Kin

The dungeon, carved deep into the island's bedrock, was dark and cavernous. As soon as the guards slammed the heavy door, we scurried, like frightened mice, into the relative safety of a dark corner and took in our surroundings. Visibility was poor – the only light a single beam that entered through an open shaft, impossibly distant, high above the dungeon floor. I worked out we were in the first of what looked like a series of vaulted chambers, one leading into the other by way of arches. It was clear that a creature had been here recently. The decaying picked-over carcasses of what looked to me like a sheep, two pigs and a cow littered the floor and created a suffocating stench. I looked to the far end of the chamber and into the next. All was quiet, but beyond that I knew not what we would find.

As I untied Amaleh's wrists and loosened her gag she looked as vulnerable as I had ever seen her and when, impulsively, I drew her close, she did not pull away. Her head rested on my shoulder and, despite our predicament, for one brief moment, I felt deeply content. After a while she appeared to recover and told me what she knew about the Dragon of Remilia. It seemed that Count Veldspar had used both Amaleh's power and the Amulet to conjure up this abominable creature from the 'Darkness', wherever that was. When I asked her, she shuddered.

'It is nowhere and everywhere. It is desolate and …' she paused.

'And,' I prompted.

'Exciting,' she finished, and she turned her head in shame.

'I cannot kill this creature, Bandred. I am too weak. There is only one way ahead and that is to overpower it.'

'But how can we do that?' I asked.

She sighed. 'I must absorb its power. Its evil must become part of me so that I can control it.'

I went to speak, then decided against it, but a fierce battle raged inside my head. My instinct was telling me not to allow her to confront such danger. I did not want to lose her again. But deep down, I knew it was the only chance we had. If the Kingdoms were to be saved, we must escape this prison soon. So I asked how I could help.

'Bait the dragon, Bandred. Bring it here. I will prepare myself.'

As I left, Amaleh was kneeling in the shaft of light, reciting a spell and raising her arms to draw in light and energy from all around. I walked away and into the darkness of the adjoining chamber wondering what I would find.

I knew that as a dragon it would not have a highly developed sense of smell, so it was unlikely the Dragon of Remilia would be aware of our presence yet. If I were to bait it, I would have to be seen, and unfortunately that meant getting close enough to put myself in danger. After what Amaleh had told me about this creature, the idea was terrifying, but we were up against time and I could think of no other way. At this very moment, Count Veldspar was flying back to Villiandra with a considerably more powerful army of dragons than those he had unleashed on us during his last attack. I thought of my dear brother, Alvah, and how I had failed him. He had warned me about Lord Dedren and I had not listened. I hoped desperately that we could escape and provide him with support.

The light was very faint now and as I walked into the fourth chamber I stumbled. Beneath me was what looked like the coiled tail of a rat. My eyes followed the coils, which rapidly grew thicker and thicker, and then along the creature's broad back. It had voluminous wings and smooth shiny scales, and a crest along its head. I had never before seen a sleeping dragon. It looked so peaceful lying there with its huge belly rising and falling, only the tips of its fangs jutting out over its lower lip hinted at the menace that lay beneath.

Without delay I positioned myself for a quick escape and bellowed at the creature as loudly as I could. The sound echoed around the chamber and immediately the dragon opened its eyes. Seeing me standing in front of it, it drew in a breath. I knew what was coming next and, running to take cover, flattened myself against a wall. A fierce blast of fire shot past me, singeing my hair and crackling as it hit the dusty floor. As soon as the flames died down, I ran. From chamber to chamber I flew, retracing my steps and hoping Amaleh was prepared. I could feel the ground tremble as the dragon followed, not once daring to look behind, I ran back into the first chamber where I drew into the shadows and waited for it to arrive.

As the Dragon of Remilia thundered in, I could see it was angry, but Amaleh, standing in the shaft of light, her arms outstretched, seemed indestructible. All of a sudden, the creature charged towards her. I held my breath, but as it approached, it slowed down, sniffing the air as if sensing something strange. Then the most extraordinary thing happened. Towering above her, the imposing creature sat. Amaleh remained calm. Soon, though, the dragon started to rave and roar, throwing its head from side to side in fury and breathing out hot shafts of fire that bounced angrily back from Amaleh's protective shield. Amaleh remained steadfast and responded by raising her arms ever higher into the air. Still the dragon spat and stamped. Still she held her ground. Then, as the dragon worked itself into its final frenzy, suddenly, from its mouth, a violent stream of thick black vapour shot forth, breaking the shield and entering Amaleh's sphere. My heart stopped, but she did not fall. Instead she simply opened her mouth and let the dark vapour flood in. When the last had disappeared, Amaleh cried out and fell to the floor. I instinctively rushed forward, still half expecting the dragon to attack. But it did not. Instead it crouched down and bowed its head low in reverence. When Amaleh arose, I sensed the change. The peace that she had exuded moments earlier had gone and in its place was power and a fathomless darkness that would forever cast a shadow over her soul.

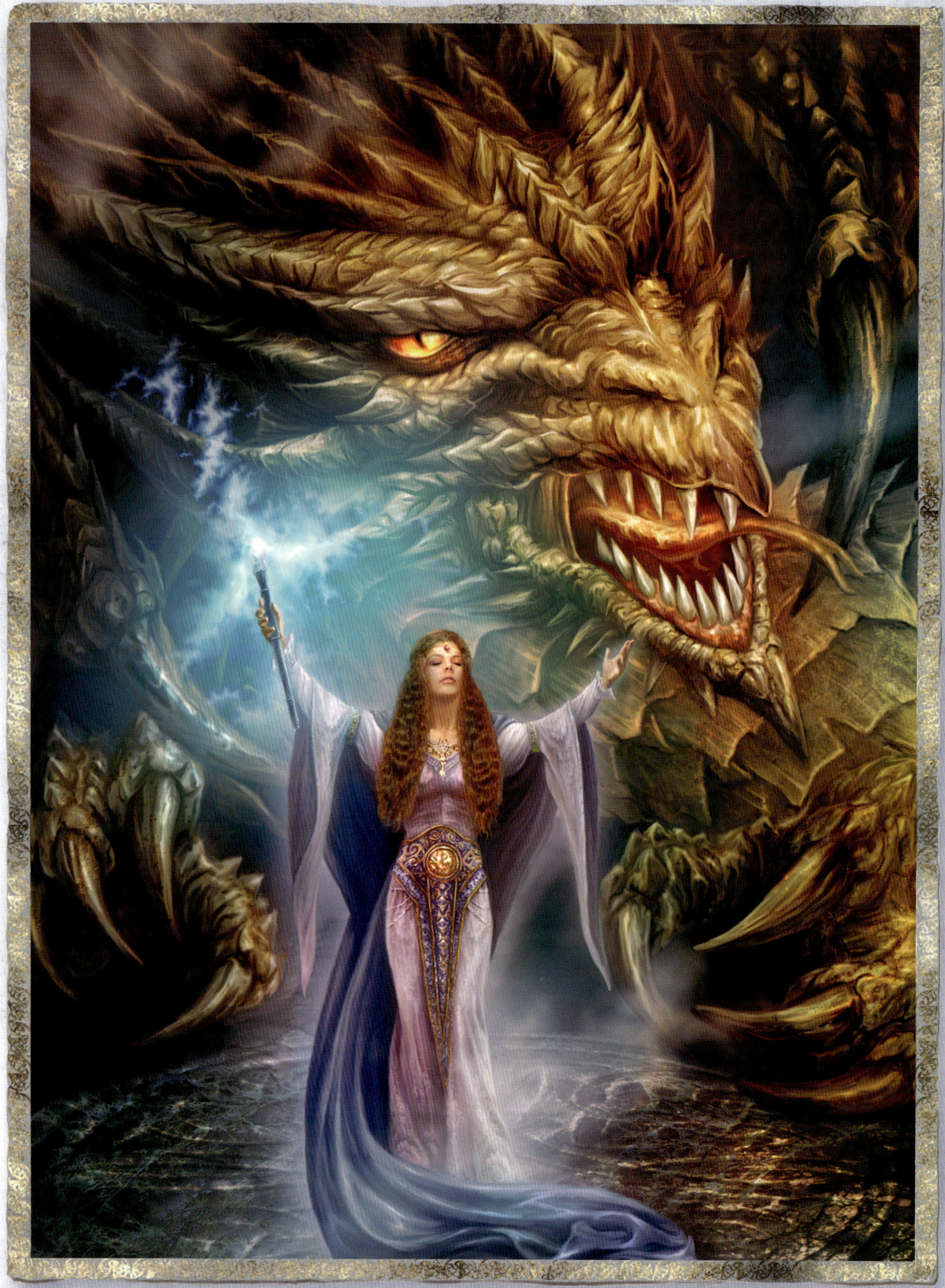

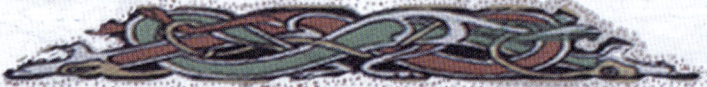

The Spell

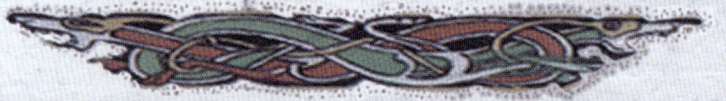

With no time to lose we climbed onto the back of the Dragon of Remilia and held tightly onto the shafts of its huge horns. Amaleh ordered it upwards and immediately it obeyed her command. Gingerly it flapped its vast wings and lifting us up with a final jerk, it flew, into the shaft of light and up towards its source. Suddenly we were free. Flying with speed through the air – towards Villiandra and our fate – whatever that might be.

We travelled for what seemed like hours, across the wide expanse of the sea. It was an exhilarating experience. We were free, together and I was returning to Villiandra. Looking down on the world gave me a different perspective and I remember feeling hopeful. But as we approached the palace, the sky darkened and we flew into a storm. A bolt of lightning crackled, just catching the dragon's wings, and for a moment or two we were thrown off course as the creature struggled to regain its balance. In the distance I could see my home, such as it was in its ruinous state. From time to time lit up by fiery blasts, I could see that the battle had already begun. As we drew closer I noticed that Alvah was leading the garrison, which was on foot and doing all it could to defend the palace against Lord Dedren's army and the onslaught of Count Veldspar's vicious dragons from above. As we advanced, the dragons, having already laid claim to the towers, were stationed in prime position, shooting rapid shafts of fire down onto the weary soldiers below. One by one they left their posts and swooping downwards plucked up soldiers, which they then used as missiles on the garrison below.

Realising I could offer little help, I turned my attention to the task of finding Count Veldspar, as without the Amulet we were fighting a losing battle. Rapidly my eyes scanned the air and soon the search was rewarded. In the midst of all the darkness, a glimmering, glistening beacon shone out – the Labyrinthine Dragon, harnessed, with Count Veldspar astride. Our dragon, by now eager to join the fray, roared loudly, and coursed forwards towards the shining pair. I realised that our only chance of defeat was a surprise attack and, thankfully, they had not spotted us yet. Amaleh urged the Dragon of Remilia onwards, commanding it to fly faster and faster until soon we were close enough to see the Amulet hanging from Count Veldspar's neck. Although he had not spotted us, many other dragons had and we were heavily under attack. Amaleh worked her magic, shooting out bolts of white light, which stunned them long enough for us to continue with our plan. Count Veldspar seemed to be laughing, clearly confident that the numerous casualties on the ground indicated the battle was almost over.

As soon as we were close enough, Amaleh commanded the Dragon of Remilia upwards so that in moments we were only a short distance above the Labyrinthine Dragon. Count Veldspar spotted us then, but before he could work out what to do, I leapt and, falling, landed awkwardly some distance from Count Veldspar on the Labyrinthine Dragon's back. As I did so, the creature felt the impact. It reared and I slid backwards, only narrowly avoiding a fall by grasping a tail spike. Slowly, and with much effort, I made my way towards the Count.

Count Veldspar, aware of his predicament and clearly shocked by this move, was ordering the dragon to thrash around. But he could not avoid me now and, as soon as I was close enough, I leapt at him, taking his neck in my hands and closing them over his windpipe. As I felt him weaken, I released my grip and grasping the Amulet, tore it from his neck. The dragon lurched and we both tumbled onto its huge wing. I looked for Amaleh, concerned that perhaps she had not been able to keep up, but she and the Dragon of Remilia were beneath us. I threw her the Amulet and it spun round, momentarily lighting up the air through which it moved. Amaleh caught it and called to me, 'Jump, Bandred,' she urged, 'Now.' But it was impossible. Count Veldspar was holding my leg and would not let go.

'Don't wait, Amaleh,' I shouted, 'do what you must.' Looking at me with a respect I knew I had come a long way to earn, she nodded. Then turning her dragon round and sitting astride with the Amulet held in front of her, Amaleh charged towards us. I looked down. We were directly above the South Tower. And so, with a final heave, I managed to pull Count Veldspar with me, off the creature and towards the ramparts below. We landed heavily on the ground and for a few moments both lay there, winded, our eyes locked in anticipation of what would happen next.

Suddenly, an extraordinarily bright light shot out from the Amulet and raced towards the Labyrinthine Dragon. As it struck its mark the creature was charged with energy, lighting up the sky with a crackling vibration so bright I had to shield my eyes. And then, as quickly as it had materialised, it disappeared, turning into a shimmering mist that wound a trail higher and higher into the sky until finally it was out of view.

Jubilant, I turned back to Count Veldspar, but he had gone. I ran down into the heart of the palace in search of him, knowing that if we were to secure our peace, he must not survive. I scanned the scene, my eyes desperately trying to seek the man my hands were eager to destroy. As I broke into the courtyard, I noticed Amaleh had demounted and was standing inside a magic circle. Flat in her palm, she held the Amulet. Her eyes were upturned and she was chanting an incantation. Then, slowly, she took her hand away. The Amulet hovered before her and a beam of pure white light flowed from her mouth towards it where, splitting into a multitude of separate shafts, each found its target in one of the dragons, including that which Count Veldspar rode. I watched as the dragon and its rider fell onto the rocks, their bodies savaged. We had won, the evil had been destroyed. I felt elation beyond words.

It was then I saw Alvah. A cheer had gone up amongst the soldiers; our enemies knew they had been defeated and many were freely giving up their weapons, flinging themselves, exhausted, on the ground. I saw Alvah's face – so proud beneath the dirt of war. He had led his men well and had proved himself to be a great warrior. I walked towards him to celebrate his brave deeds. It was then that I spotted Lord Dedren approaching from the side. I shouted, but so loud were the cheers of jubilation he could not hear my call. And so I watched. Watched as a man full with years of bitter envy unleashed his wrath on my brother. Pushing through the celebrating men I caught Alvah as he fell and dropped to the floor with him. He looked so young, so alive lying there with his head in my arms, even though the blood drained from the great wound in the side of his body.

'Alvah, I . . .'

'Go, Bandred,' his words were slow and clearly difficult to speak, 'for the safety of your Kingdoms, destroy that man.'

I kissed his hand and feeling the life draining out of him, turned and flew with fury in the direction Lord Dedren had made his escape. Dodging the still-celebrating crowd, I spotted his dark figure slip out of the southern tower door. In great leaps I descended the Hundred Steps Passage. I had never felt so alive. I was full of fury and, if I had caught Lord Dedren at that moment, I would have torn him limb from limb. It wasn't until I reached the beach that I saw he was not alone.

Lord Dedren was wielding a sword high above Amaleh, who was gagged and tied to a rock. In his free hand, he held the Amulet. I hesitated for a moment and, before I knew what was happening, was jumped on from behind, dragged face down in the sand and forced to kneel at Lord Dedren's feet.

'So glad you've arrived,' snarled Lord Dedren. 'I think our sorceress needs a little inspiration. Perhaps you're the one who can provide it.' And he nodded to his men.

Two of them pulled me backwards by the arms, whilst the other placed a blade to my throat. I felt a drop of blood trickle down my neck.

'Leave him!' screamed Amaleh.

'Perhaps you will help me now,' said Lord Dedren.

'Whatever you want,' she said quietly.

'The Labyrinthine Dragon, of course,' said Lord Dedren.

The guards untied Amaleh and Lord Dedren handed her the Amulet.

'Do not think of tricking us,' he barked, 'it will only take a moment for King Bandred to die.'

Holding the Amulet in the palm of her hand, I watched as Amaleh, for a second time, chanted the materialisation spell. Unlike before when she had used the Orb, this time the dragon appeared quickly, rushing towards us from the sky in a shimmering trail of dust before solidifying into its magnificent form.

Slowly I inched my eyes to look at the captor on my left. Although he gripped my arm, my hand was just inches away from the sword attached to his belt – if I could just take them by surprise. I stared at Amaleh, trying to indicate my intent. She returned my gaze and at that moment turned the Amulet away from the dragon and towards my captors. A bright light shot out, blinding them for a second and I took my chance, flinging my head and neck backwards away from the bare blade, I used my full weight to pull my captors down. In the struggle I managed to seize the sword and brandishing it about, kept the attackers at bay.

A little way off, I saw Lord Dedren grab the Amulet and throw Amaleh to the ground, gripping her arm to keep her from escaping. The dragon, sensing menace in the air and without guidance from the Amulet,

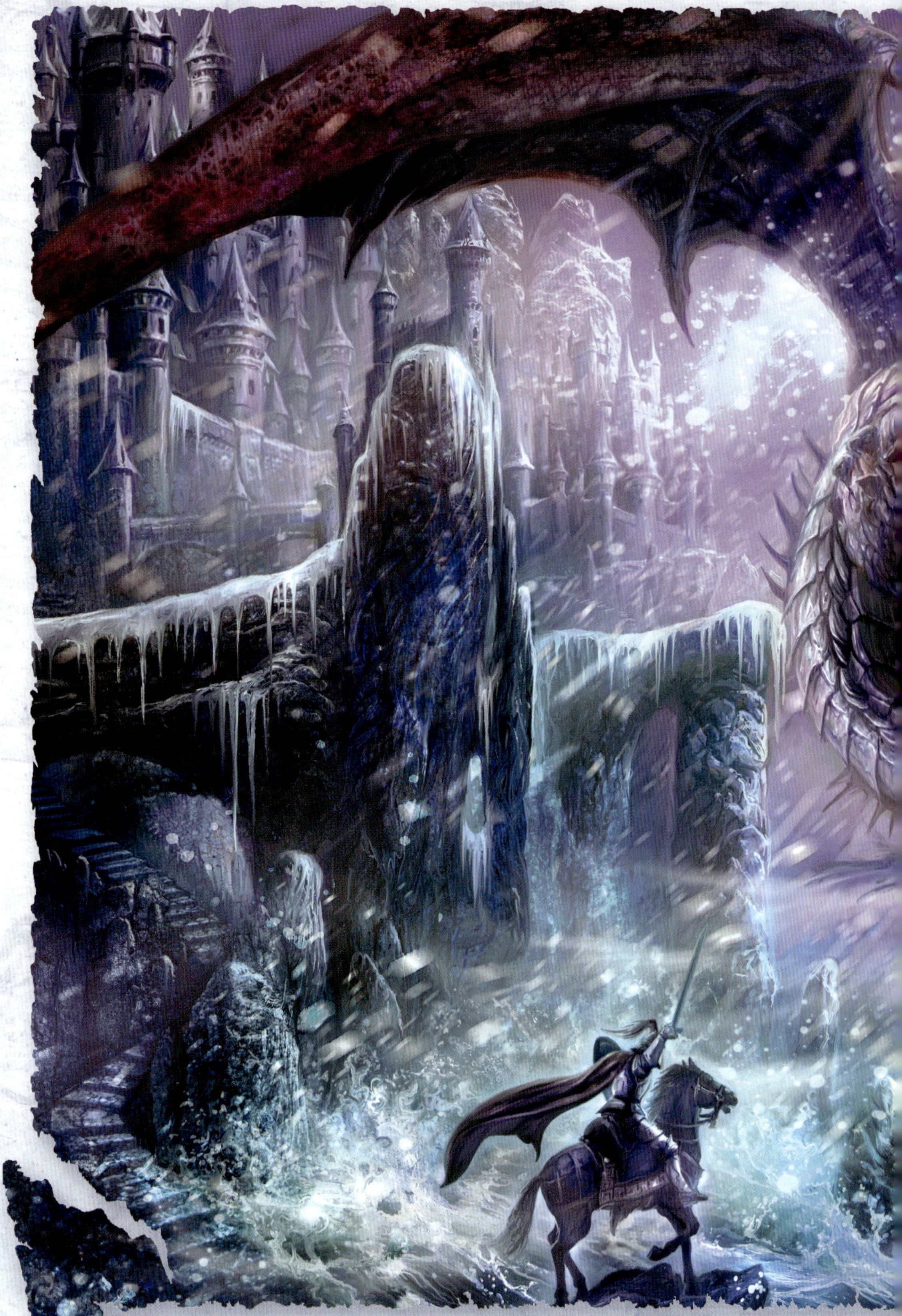

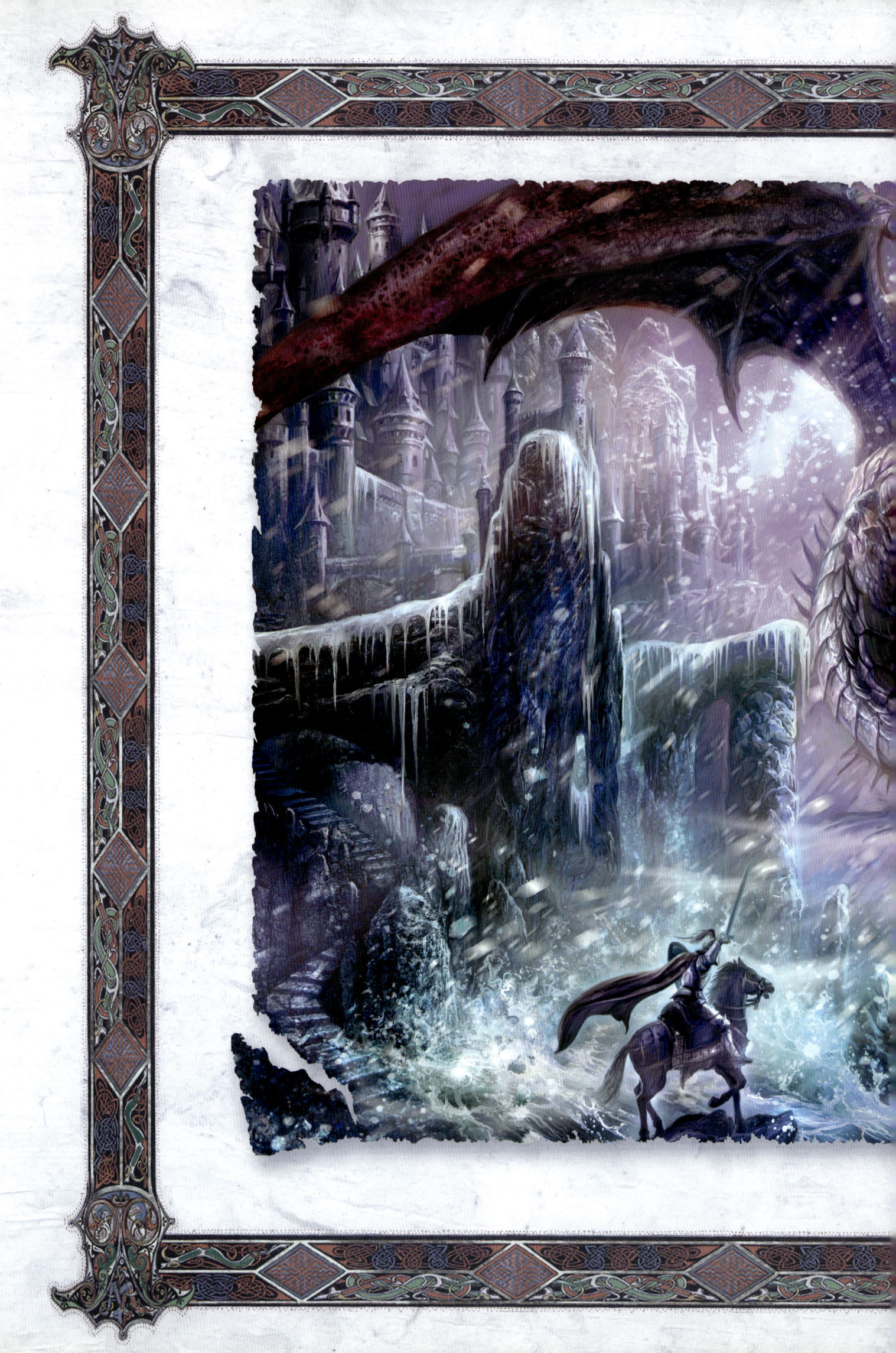

Dragon Attack!

started to snort hot blasts of fire towards the couple before swooping up into the air. But Lord Dedren would not let her go. I could see that if they did not run soon, they would both be killed. I was desperate to reach Amaleh.

Then I heard her scream. Her robe was on fire and huge licks of burning flames were working their way up her body. Lord Dedren jumped away, there was little that he could do now. I knew I must act now or we would all be lost. Spinning the sword in my outstretched arm, I moved towards her, my adversaries finding it impossible to get close. As soon as I was in reach, I hurled myself on top of Amaleh, my body and the sand beneath dampening the flames. I looked up to see the Labyrinthine Dragon returning, breathing out a vast wall of fire as it flew along the length of the beach. Swiftly, I picked up Amaleh and ran towards the forest to take cover. But Lord Dedren, startled by my rescue, had not noticed the dragon's return. He seemed rooted to the spot. The dragon's blast, when it came, engulfed his body and in an instant he was burning from head to foot. Screaming with pain and staggering towards the sea, Lord Dedren dropped just short of the water, the dreadful smell of his charred body drifting towards us on the sea breeze.

'The Amulet,' cried Amaleh. 'I must get it back. The dragon must be controlled.' And she ran out onto the beach again. Terrified for her safety, I watched with anticipation as Amaleh scoured the ground. In the distance I could see that the dragon had spotted her and was making its return.

'Hurry,' I cried. But she was determined to find it. Then suddenly I heard a piercing shriek and the dragon's body recoiled in the air. Looking back to Amaleh, I could see the Amulet hovering before her, a single white shaft of light streaming from the jewel towards the immense creature. Then Amaleh, using the Amulet as a channel for her magical powers, guided the shimmering creature to the ground. Once in front of her it knelt, bowing its head low. After a while, Amaleh lowered the Amulet, walked towards the dragon and gently touched its nose. I rushed towards her with the elation of one knowing that immediate danger had passed, but I was unprepared for what was coming.

'Farewell, King Bandred,' she said, mounting the dragon. 'You saved my life. The evil that has troubled the Kingdoms has been defeated. We have proved a formidable team.'

'Don't go, Amaleh,' I pleaded. 'Stay here with us for some while longer.'

'You have little need of me now,' she replied. 'Your people have seen you succeed – you have earned their respect, the palace will be restored and the cities will slowly regain their prosperity. It is time now for me to return to my home.'

I looked at her and saw the darkness behind her eyes. My heart reached out and she felt it, responding with the words, 'It is nothing but a memory of ourselves for which we yearn, Bandred,' and I knew she was right. We had changed, we were different now, and so I let her go.